Seasons of Time

featuring

The Cross Poem

Seasons of Time

featuring
The Cross Poem

Depicting the Crucifixion
from the viewpoint of the Cross

from the author of
"Adventures in Thackerville"

Steven R. Thacker

authorHOUSE®

AuthorHouse™
1663 Liberty Drive
Bloomington, IN 47403
www.authorhouse.com
Phone: 1-800-839-8640

Published by AuthorHouse   07/20/2012

ISBN: 978-1-4685-7666-5 (sc)
ISBN: 978-1-4685-7667-2 (e)

Library of Congress Control Number: 2012906211

DEDICATION: This book is dedicated to my loving wife, Debby Jo. It is she who has been truly the love of my life and my closest and dearest friend. There has been no one (with the exception of my dear sweet Lord) that has been such a blessing to my life as she.

Disclaimer:

All information covered in this material is by the Author. It is not the intention of the Author to copy works by another. There is a tendency to "accidentally" recall poems by others and they could find their way into the material not realizing it at the time. If this occurs, it is not the intention of the Author.

CONTENTS

SECTION 1

SECTION 2

SECTION 3

SECTION 4

SECTION 1

LONG POEMS
Featuring
'The Cross Poem'

THE CROSS

My roots grew along the Jordan's bank,
It seemed I could touch the sky;
My shade stretched across the sand,
Where the Savior once passed by.

Then one day a soldier strong,
Stood in front of me;
With axe in hand he viewed my trunk,
As straight as it could be.

He began to cut my life away,
I can still recall the sound;
Of steel as it cut at my side,
And soon I was upon the ground.

He cut the shade from off my head,
Then loaded me upon his cart;
That's when I learned the frightening news,
That broke my wooden heart.

They made of me a rugged wooden cross,
With splinters in every crack;
Then they picked me up and laid me on,
The Savior's bleeding back.

The weight of me was so great,
He fell beneath the load;
So, the soldiers grabbed another man,
To carry me up that road.

When on the hill the Lord laid,
Upon my wooden back;
They nailed His hands, then His feet,
I thought my wood would crack.

~ Steven R. Thacker ~

Then they lifted up my mighty frame,
And dropped it into a hole;
And then they laughed and jeered at Christ,
As He hung there all alone.

I heard Him forgive a thief,
Who hung on a cross nearby;
I felt the tears roll down His cheeks,
As He saw His mother cry.

I heard Him say, "It is finished",
As He gave a tender sigh;
Then I felt my Creator,
Drop His head and die.

They took Him off my cross of wood,
And placed Him in a tomb;
But three days later, He came back,
As He conquered death's chains of gloom.

Now, when I remember back,
To when the Savior died that day;
I'm not ashamed, but rather proud,
Of the roll I had to play.

When all the world had let Him down,
I held Him high above the land;
When all had left His side,
I held His bleeding hands.

So, I'm not ashamed of the part I played,
As Christ's blood fell upon the land;
I'm just an old rugged wooden cross,
Who had a part in the Master's plan.

1982

~ Steven R. Thacker ~

COME ON HOME FAITHFUL SERVANT

You gave the Lord your life,
So many years ago;
Though storms would come to you,
The weak would never know.

You always stood for Jesus,
In a time when others fell;
You proved your love in many ways,
More oft than tongue could tell.

So, come on home faithful servant,
Your work on earth is done;
Come on home faithful servant,
Your race on earth is run.

They'll be no pain nor sorrow,
And your mansion's already done;
Come on home faithful servant,
And meet God's only Son.

All the burdens here below,
You carried with delight;
As you held close to the Word of God,
And stood for what was right.

I learned a lot from you,
Of how a man should stand for God;
And how the battle is the Lord's,
And not for man's applause.

~ Steven R. Thacker ~

So, come on home faithful servant,
Your work on earth is done;
Come on home faithful servant,
Your race on earth is run.
They'll be no pain nor sorrow,
And your mansion's already done;
Come on home faithful servant,
And meet God's only Son.

Though tears my fill our eyes,
And our hearts may grieve inside;
We know you're in a better place,
With Jesus at your side.

So, while you're up in glory,
And we travel here below;
We'll finish our course with gladness,
And, we'll see you again we know.

1990 In Honor of Grandma, Cora Edith Courtright Weaver, Wheelersburg, OH

~ Steven R. Thacker ~

OUR FLAG

America is the land I love,
The land of liberty;
A place where one can serve his God,
For all the world to see.

I marvel at the patriots true,
Who gather near us here;
Who placed themselves in perils grasp,
For the land they loved so dear.

When my eyes behold Old Glory,
As she waves in autumn's wind;
I feel the tears flow down my cheeks,
As I gaze at my old friend.

Our flag is more than ink and thread,
In colors of red, white and blue;
It represents a Nation great,
And a people that are free and true.

It stands for all the countless throng,
Who bled on foreign sod;
They bravely fought the battle strong,
For this Nation under God.

I know at times our leaders,
Have departed from God's design;
But we must not give up the fight,
For God's will we must define.

This flag that stands for country strong,
Shall always wave we pray;
'Til all the battles have been fought,
And we're home with God to stay.

So, wave Old Glory and make us proud,
May your colors forever fly;
And stand for peace and liberty,
In remembrance for those who died.

05/29/94 The Nation that forgets her warriors will one day herself be forgotten.

~ Steven R. Thacker ~

THE TRACKS

I remember when I was just a boy,
And we lived by a railroad track;
I used to play upon those rails,
As my mind remembers back.

I recall the endless rails,
And the spikes that held them there;
The railroad cars all loaded down,
Could travel with such care.

For the rails would stand the test of time,
While the trains would come and go;
So too is Jesus like the rail,
His Grace forever flows.

He too was nailed with spikes one day,
In His hands and in His feet;
But spikes were not what held Him there,
He was there for sins defeat.

Our sin had placed Him on that cross,
But His love beyond compare;
Would keep Him on that cross of shame,
For He knew He must stay there.

So, when my thoughts go back in time,
And I see that endless track;
I think of God's own precious Son,
With stripes upon His back.

Who paid the price for all my sin,
And set my spirit free;
And finished God's redemptive plan,
Upon that cruel tree.

So, when you see a railroad track,
And the spikes that hold them there;
Perhaps you'll think of Calvary,
And that love beyond compare.

12/16/2006

~ Steven R. Thacker ~

THE BOOK OF BOOKS

There's a Book that we hold to,
That grips the souls of men;
It's stood the test of all the years,
And will guide a life from sin.

But though this Book can feed our souls,
And lead to God's own Grace;
It won't do any good at all,
When neglected in its place.

There are books that enhance our learning,
And books to stronger wealth;
There are books to improve our beauty,
And books to enhance our health.

Man in his lofty thoughts,
Has helped the world we see;
But only that which is from above,
Can set the captive free.

The lost would construct a stairway,
To reach to Heaven's throne;
But when they climb those steps of man,
They'll find they're all alone.

For steps to God can't be found,
Within the schemes of man;
For only in the Book of God,
Can be found the Master's plan.

That plan must start at Calvary,
And lead to an empty tomb;
And then through humble faith in Christ,
Will that soul be free from Satan's doom.

So, the Book of books that we need the most,
Is the one not designed by man;
But the one from God's own heart,
And written by God's own hand.

01/07/2007

~ Steven R. Thacker ~

WOULD I BE A HELPING HAND?

If I would chance one day to see,
A beggar all alone;
Would I be willing in my heart,
To take him to my home?

If he were wounded deep within,
And sin had gripped his heart;
Would I be willing, Oh Lord, I pray,
To simply do my part?

Would I but try to do God's will,
And try his soul to win?
Or would I say, "be warmed and filled,"
And send him out again?

Please help me see the broken, Lord,
That pass by me each day;
And help me, God, to show to them,
Your truth from these lips of clay.

The broken that stand about us,
They need a helping hand;
And only the peace that God can give,
Can save from sin's sinking sand.

Oh, help me, Lord, remember,
That once I was broken too;
I thank You, God, for those helping hands,
That brought me safe to You.

I think too of the brother,
Who in a time of stress;
Could use these helping hands of mine,
To show Your gentleness.

So, when we see a need,
The Lord needs us to stand;
And do our part and show our love,
By lending a helping hand.
09/29/1995

~ Steven R. Thacker ~

WHO AM I?

I reached for the mountains,
That rose to the sky;
I reached for the world's rainbows,
That were lofty and high.

I followed my ambitions,
And was never too shy;
I was climbing for life's victories,
Do you know—who am I?

I am always in a hurry,
No one else can be the best;
I run for the first place,
Ahead of all the rest.

I want for great treasures,
Whether I cheat, steal or lie;
Do I have you wondering?
Now think real hard,—who am I?

I came to a crossroads,
In my travels through this land;
Do I take the one of worldly pleasures,
Or the one of the nail pierced hands?

With tears in my eyes,
And conviction in my heart;
I fell on my face for mercy,
Then for the cross I made my start.

My journey has not been easy,
As I met the Devil face to face;
I think you know my secret,
I'm only a sinner, saved by grace.

1981

~ Steven R. Thacker ~

I WONDER

I wonder what will be the scene,
When at God's judgment bar;
All those violators of His Word,
Are shown for what they are.

They've lied about creation,
And about the fall of man;
They've lied about salvations need,
And about the Father's plan.

But those lies that they have written,
That had caused some weak to fall;
Will greet them in God's Heaven,
When the Savior gives forth His call.

For all will stand before Him,
And report what they have done;
A life of faithful service,
Or rebellion to His Son.

But the ones who've altered scripture,
To suit their sinful pride;
Will find that at the bar of God,
They'll have no place to hide.

And when they stand before Him,
They will see His Book so clear;
They'll see their words aren't present,
And it's His words they must hear.

So, change it if you want to,
And ignore God's written plan;
But be sure one day you'll think differently,
When before the Judge you stand.

12/17/2009

~ Steven R. Thacker ~

WHEN LIFE HAS TURNED
THE PAGE

When life has turned its final page,
And you must say goodbye;
What will you think as you look back,
Will you laugh or will you cry?

Will there be victories lost to you,
In that race that you would not try?
Or that life of service you could have had,
But you claimed you were shy?

What friendships did you make in life,
Did you make a difference here?
How did you walk within your home,
Did they know that your love was near?

I pray that you will fill with joy,
As you consider then;
And know that you were right with God,
And not regret what could have been.

For it's not about the trophies,
Or the ribbons in the case;
And it's not about the cheers of man,
Within the human race.

True joy and peace is only found,
When you leave this earthly place;
And when you lay this body down,
And see the Savior's face.

~ Steven R. Thacker ~

For when this walk on earth is done,
And our journey is complete;
We'll take the crowns that we have won,
And cast at Jesus feet.

But sad would be that day,
As we stand on that golden sand;
And face the precious Son of God,
With not but empty hands.

So, run with joy this race below,
And serve with all your heart;
For when He comes to take you home,
It will be too late to start.

03/05/2007

~ Steven R. Thacker ~

ABIDE

Many are they that watch the fight,
Of we who stand for God;
They see us battle against the foe,
As we must onward trod.

My heart grows sad as I think,
Of the few they see that flee;
They can't abide the battle strong,
Too often it's these they see.

Why can't the army of our Lord,
Their captain more clearly see;
If they would behold His wounded frame,
Would they more faithful be?

When I but think of those precious hands,
That held a child so dear;
Was nailed in anger by that one,
Without a falling tear.

When I recall the voice that day,
As He calmed a troubled sea;
Ask for water from the cross,
As He died for you and me.

I cannot leave His wounded side,
As we battle Satan's host;
For I could never give enough,
To my Lord who gave the most.

So, take a stand, dear child of God,
And never leave His side;
For He will give the strength you need,
As you each day abide.

1991

~ Steven R. Thacker ~

IN YOUR MIND RECALL

My mind goes back to Calvary,
Where Jesus died for me;
They shed His blood and pierced His side,
As He set the captives free.

When burdens overshadow,
And heartaches grip my soul;
I recall that rugged cross,
Where Jesus made me whole.

Though steep may be the mountains,
That I must surely climb;
There's just one thing that comforts me,
I know that victory's mine.

So, when this world would buffet,
Your small and feeble frame;
Be sure that you can always,
Call upon His name.

For if His words can calm the storm,
And His power can heal the blind;
Then He can hold your trembling hand,
And love you all the time.

So, in your mind recall that day,
When Jesus set you free;
When He saw your pain and knew your hurt,
As he died on Calvary.

Yes, my mind goes back to Calvary,
Where Jesus died for me;
Where they shed His blood and pierced His side,
As He set this captive free.

01/29/2007

~ Steven R. Thacker ~

I CLOSE MY EYES

I close my eyes and dream of life,
With wings beneath my feet;
I run, and leap and jump for joy,
In a life that's full and sweet.

I see me soar with eagles,
And fly among the stars;
But then my eyes awaken,
And I view life's restricting bars.

I once again climb from my bed,
To face another day;
I start my day by asking God,
To take my hurt away.

Each day is filled with struggles,
As I try to walk aright;
I must endure my handicap,
In the day and in the night.

But then I lay my head once more,
Upon my pillow true;
And let my mind take journey's ride,
On wings beyond the blue.

I close my eyes and dream of life,
With wings beneath my feet;
I run, and leap and jump for joy,
In a life that's full and sweet.

I see me soar with eagles,
And fly among the stars;
But then my eyes awaken,
And I view life's restricting bars.

~ Steven R. Thacker ~

Now in my bedroom close to me,
Is my family all around;
They stand a silent vigil,
But no ease can there be found.

They want to give me comfort,
To ease my troubled mind;
But they don't seem to realize,
Real peace I soon will find.

The next time when my eyes awaken,
And from this bed I flee;
I won't be bound by sickness here,
For Christ shall set me free.

I'll run upon the sands of God,
Beside the crystal sea;
I'll soar the eagle's lofty height,
In that land where God takes me.

The heartache that this world affords,
Matters little when life is done;
The peace I have is clearly seen,
In Isaiah forty, verse thirty-one.

01/5/2007

~ Steven R. Thacker ~

NO TIME

Instant coffee,
Instant tea;
An instant life,
Now, that's for me.

I want it now,
And don't be late;
There's one thing sure,
I just can't wait.

I want to walk,
The heavenly way;
As long as it comes,
Without delay.

I want to grow,
In God's grace divine;
But make it quick,
I've not much time.

To serve the Lord,
And be faithful and true;
That's just not for me,
I've too much to do.

Now if this is you,
Dear friend of mine;
When it comes to God,
And you haven't much time.

Be sure the day,
Will soon appear;
When God's own hand,
Will draw you near.

He'll ask of you,
Like that servant of old;
"Just what happened,

~ Steven R. Thacker ~

To that talent of gold?"

Then you will say,
With a shivering sound;
"I took what you gave,
And hid it in the ground."

"I did not invest,
In your work divine;
For you see, dear Lord,
I didn't make time."

"No time for the Bible,
I often heard read;
No time for the Church,
Where God's people were fed."

"No time for a lifestyle,
That would honor Your name;
No money for tithing,
But plenty for gain."

"I shared with the world,
That joke from within;
But never a witness,
So their soul I might win."

May God help us ponder,
That talent within;
And use it for God's glory,
And not waste it on sin.

So, help us, Lord, to remember,
With your wisdom so sublime;
That when it comes to serving You,
We should always find the time.
09/03/95

~ Steven R. Thacker ~

GOD'S SPECIAL GIFT

God has blessed this life of mine,
In many special ways;
But one that stands before the rest,
Is a mother's loving gaze.

God gave to me a Grandmother,
Whose standards became my own;
She taught me of God's wondrous ways,
In the things that are seen, felt and known.

She gave to me a tender heart,
That would weep and often sigh;
Perhaps because of autumns leaves,
Or a puppy that would die.

God gave to me a Mother,
Whose ways were strong and true;
Who often saw starvation's face,
But she brought her family through.

She taught to me that persistence,
Would often be the key;
The key that opened up the door,
To a life of victory.

My Grandmother and my Mother,
Would show of Jesus' love;
And how with His almighty hand,
This child could live above.

They taught me that, though often times,
This world was cold and bare;
That if you pushed aside all doubt,
The love of Christ was there.

~ Steven R. Thacker ~

Now I must say that though these two,
Are heroes to my life;
God has also blessed this little boy,
With a loving and faithful wife.

For I see in her all the strengths,
Of those who walked before;
A guiding and loving force,
Of our children and so much more.

She was always there when tumbled child,
Would have a wounded knee;
She wiped the tears and hugged the neck,
And soon a smile she'd see.

And when the children left our home,
And went their separate ways;
They took with them a godly past,
Of a mother's love and those happy days.

She taught them how to reach for God,
When they were small and frail;
She taught them how a Savior's love,
Would never, ever fail.

I praise the Lord for Mothers true,
And their watch both day and night;
For theirs is such a godly task,
Of a course that's pure and right.

My wife to me is so much more,
Then words from a poets pen;
She's God's special gift to a little boy,
Who's happier than he's ever been.

1998

~ Steven R. Thacker ~

OBSOLETE

This body that I'm housed in,
Has been just fine for me;
It carried all my hurts and pains,
On this we must agree.

But in that life beyond the grave,
When I my Lord shall meet;
This shell that has done so well,
Will then be obsolete.

These eyes that need assistance,
To study and to know;
Will not be then up to the task,
Of what Heaven's scenes will show.

These ears that listened to the world,
And those things opposed to peace;
Will then be listening to precious things,
As angelic cords release.

These legs that often struggle,
As I strive to cross a room;
Will run, and leap, and jump for joy,
Beyond this world of gloom.

Those feet that often stumbled,
As I've tried to make my way;
Will one day walk on golden streets,
In that land of the endless day.

No, this body that I'm housed in,
And the one that you would greet;
One day must be left behind,
For it will then be obsolete.

09/20/09

~ Steven R. Thacker ~

THE BATTLE IS THE LORD'S

When my heart would grieve inside,
By those who trouble me;
I may wish to find a way,
That others might also see.

I want to fight and prove my case,
So others would support my life;
To hold my head and wipe my brow,
And uphold me in my strife.

But proof and guidance in this life,
Is not what my heart needs;
To give the type of grace and joy,
And take this hurt from me.

When Satan attacks the believer,
And trouble would come our way;
It's easy to view the enemy,
As those who pass each day.

We then must look beyond this realm,
And see through spiritual eyes;
That we battle not with flesh and blood,
But with one who seeks a prize.

For the Devil seeks to battle God,
And to defeat His children true;
But he cannot hope to win over God,
Except through me and you.

So, when you're faced with the enemy,
Just know that you must trust;
For it's not about revenge and might,
It's about a God that's just.

For God will win the battle,
On this you know is true;
And those who fight the Devil's cause,
Will one day get their due.

02/24/11

~ Steven R. Thacker ~

YOU MAY HAVE

You may have great riches,
Great wealth beyond compare;
Your talents may be wondrous,
With friends in which to share.

But what will be tomorrow,
When all your health is gone;
What about your wealth that day,
Will they buy you another dawn?

Can a price be placed on Heaven,
Or a bounty be made of peace?
Can the Judge be bought or bargained with,
When the offer is only me?

No, the price was paid at Calvary,
In the life of a Savior true;
When His blood flowed down a wooden cross,
As He died for me and you.

So, riches are but fleeting,
And health will fade away;
But faith and hope in God alone,
Will lead to that endless day.

Where Christ Himself will take our hand,
And keep us in His care;
In a place where all is joy and peace,
In that land beyond compare.

03/20/07

~ Steven R. Thacker ~

YOUR NAME

It came from your father,
It was all he had to give;
So, it's yours to use and cherish,
As long as you may live.

If you lose the watch he gave you,
It can always be replaced;
But a black mark on your name, Son,
Can never be erased.

It was clean the day you took it,
And a worthy name to bear;
When you got it from your father,
There was no dishonor there.

So, make sure you guard it wisely,
After all is said and done;
You'll be glad the name is spotless,
When you give it to your son.

2005

~ Steven R. Thacker ~

SECTION 2

Poems to Touch the Heart
Calm the Fears
Challenge Your Walk with God.

FIERY TRIALS

The fiery trials of my soul,
Can often make me weak;
I only need give God control,
And pleasant pastures seek.

I find myself more oft than not,
In Satan's crafty hand;
To cause my faith to turn from God,
And step on sinking sand.

I quickly raise my eyes to Him,
Who always stands nearby;
He gently takes my trembling hand,
And whispers, "Hear am I."

Now as He leads through waters deep,
O'er every winding mile;
I strive to give to God above,
Each gruesome fiery trial.

10/09/1988

GOD'S CONTROL

A faithful life,
Should be our goal;
And it can only be found,
Within God's control.

02/19/2007

~ Steven R. Thacker ~

GOD CARES FOR ME

In the gloom,
Of my despair;
I seek to see,
If God is there.

I turn about,
With eyes that's cried;
And see my Savior,
At my side.

No matter what,
The tempest may be;
My Lord will always,
Take care of me.

2005

HOME AT LAST

I have no more pain,
And I have no more strife;
For I've trusted the Lord,
For everlasting life.

My tears are all gone,
And my sorrow is past;
I praise the Lord,
I'm home at last.

1998

~ Steven R. Thacker ~

GOD'S GRACE

The peace I needed came to me,
The day He set me free;
It was like the world was taken off,
And sweet joy was given me.

I know there are yet foes to face,
And there are heartaches still ahead;
But I know that Jesus walks with me,
For He's my living bread.

I rest each day in His loving arms,
And trust His guidance true;
For I know that whether life or death,
His grace will take me through.

05/04/2003

STEPHEN STOOD

Stephen stood for the Word of God,
And suffered for the same;
He stood the test midst angry men,
As he called on Jesus' name.

They tried to stop the words he spoke,
With rocks from off the ground;
But Stephen looked to Heaven true,
And laid his body down.

08/01/2004

~ Steven R. Thacker ~

GOD'S GIFT

God's gift was given,
In a stable one night;
And with hopeful hearts,
They beheld the sight.

The Shepherds came,
And the Angels sang;
Though the night was dark,
The courts of Heaven rang.

For the world received,
On a bed of straw;
God's beloved Son,
Who would give His all.

For this child grew up,
And followed God's plan;
To redeem the world,
And bring salvation to man.

12/12/2003

MY STEPS

My steps will be on Golden streets,
And my eyes will be on heavenly joys;
My heart will rejoice in the presence of God,
And the burdens of life will no longer annoy.

01/01/2007 Psalms 37:23

~ Steven R. Thacker ~

GOD'S GENTLE CARE

With nail pierced hands He molds my life,
And fashions with such care;
That all the world may look and see,
The peace of God that's there.

He somehow takes my broken mess,
That caused me so much grief;
And shows His love in a thousand ways,
And brings my life relief.

I praise the Lord for that fine day,
When I gave to Him my life;
For He took control of all I am,
And removed my bitter strife.

Now when I view a cloudy day,
And storms around I see;
I'll rest aboard His peaceful craft,
Where the storms cannot harm me.

Yes, the nail pierced hands that molds my life,
And fashions with such care;
Will always be my constant guide,
For I know He's always there.

1997 Psalms 27:4

LOVE BEYOND COMPARE

I can recall the moment, when Jesus redeemed my life;
He gave to me sweet joy divine, and took away my strife.

~ Steven R. Thacker ~

GOD'S PEACE

The peace of God that fills my life,
Is that which I can't explain;
It reaches to the core of me,
And scatters guilt and pain.

When life around would frighten me,
And cause my heart to dread;
My Lord would whisper, "Peace be still,
For I'm your living bread."

So, when the storms would buffet,
And fear might come my way;
I rest in His almighty care,
For He's my hope and stay.

06/06/2004 John 14:1-3

JESUS CAME TO ME

The love of Jesus came to me,
And found me lost in sin;
He showed to me my broken life,
And a longing deep within.

He took away my burden,
And He took away my pain;
He gave to me salvation,
And gave me life again.

02/10/2007

~ Steven R. Thacker ~

GRUDGES

A grudge not released,
Can only hurt me;
There will come a time,
When I should set them free.

For bitterness that's held,
Will sour my life;
And left unchecked,
Will cause hatred and strife.

So, release that grudge,
And place it in the past;
And you soon will see,
Sweet peace at last.
02/19/2007

IN GOD'S LOVING HAND

The riches of this world,
Will often bring us strife;
And the things that we possess,
Can't bring eternal life.

But in the loving hand of God,
There are wonders for us to find;
For in His presence there will be,
Joy and grace with peace of mind.
01/23/2007

~ Steven R. Thacker ~

IN THE STORM

I must take the hand of God,
And trust Him every day;
Though winds of strife would buffet me,
The Lord will be my stay.

He lets me know that He is there,
Though dark may be my trial;
He's shown His loving light to me,
Each long and dreary mile.

So, let the storms around me blow,
And let the enemy do his best;
For I have One who walks with me,
Who has always stood the test.

06/27/2004

THE BEST HE HAD

God gave to us the best He had,
To show His tender love;
A greater gift has never been,
Then our Savior from above.

12/14/2000

~ Steven R. Thacker ~

DETERMINE TO DO RIGHT

When we determine to do what is right,
We are well on our way to winning the fight.

03/28/2007

TRUST

Trust the Lord,
In all you do;
And know His grace,
Will care for you.

12/8/09

GRACE ALONE

It's all of grace and not of works,
In this you can depend;
For man to try to work to God,
Is all too foolish, my friend.

So, place your trust in Christ alone,
And put your faith in Him;
And when this life is all complete,
You'll meet your dearest friend.

He'll take you from this world of woe,
To heights beyond compare;
Your final abode will be with God,
And meet your loved ones there.

So, trust not in this world my friend,
To secure that heavenly shore;
Remember that it's Christ alone,
For He's the only door.

04/15/1998

~ Steven R. Thacker ~

HE GUIDES

The hand that guides the sparrow,
And gives the gentle rain;
Can guide our steps and lead our way,
When questions would bring pain.

At times we get too anxious,
And try to force our way;
But we should wait upon the Lord,
And see what He might say.

So, Lord, restore my patience.
And help me trust in thee;
And watch your precious hand,
Prepare your path for me.
02/11/2008

THE DARK VALLEY

Though dark may be my valley,
And shadows hide the way;
He gently takes my trembling hand,
And it's there I need to stay.

For I can't see the path ahead,
To danger I am blind;
But there's one thing that comforts me,
God's been there all the time.
02/10/2008

~ Steven R. Thacker ~

HIS CONTROL

This life affords but little peace,
When walking on our own;
Though we travel in a crowd it seems,
We still are all alone.

But there's a hand that guides my life,
And keeps me day by day;
No matter what my friends may do,
I know He'll always stay.

So, when I walk the lonesome road,
And fear would grip my soul;
I'll take Him by His loving hand,
And let His grace control.

02/15/2007

WHEN JESUS WORKS

Grief and pain will often drain,
And tear your life into;
While joy and peace will bring relief,
When Jesus works through you.

03/09/2007

~ Steven R. Thacker ~

HIS TOUCH

His hand is there to guide us,
When hearts are filled with fear;
We only need to trust His grace,
To fill that heart with cheer.

11/4/2011

HELP ME TO REMEMBER

All I need I have, dear Lord,
Within Thy grace divine;
For I could never exhaust the depths,
Of Your love so strong and kind.

Please help me find the courage, Lord,
To reach beyond my pride;
And take the hand of a drowning soul,
And lift him to where You abide.

That soul that stands in peril,
And needs someone to care;
Help me, Lord, to take your Word,
To lead, to guide, and to share.

Please help me, Lord and Master,
To never forget that day;
When a strong and loving nail-pierced hand,
Helped me on my way.

03/21/2002

~ Steven R. Thacker ~

WALK THE PATH

Walk the path that God has shown,
And strive to do your best;
For in the end when the victory's won,
We then will find our rest.

04/02/2005 Matthew 11:28

THE PEACE WE NEED

Peace of mind,
And peace of soul;
Will not be found,
In my control.

For the peace I need,
And that peace so grand;
Can only be found,
In the Master's hand.

02/19/2007

IT'S GOOD

It's good to know the people of God,
Are there to encourage me;
To know that they will truly care,
When I would heartache see.

It's good to have a church that loves,
And not a critical one;
It's nice to know that I can smile,
And even have some fun.

It's good to hear the Word of God,
With words I understand;
And it's nice to know that if I need help,
There are those who will lend a hand.

02/2001

~ Steven R. Thacker ~

HE HOLDS MY HAND

Though storms may come,
And the trials may fall;
We can rest assured,
That God is over all.

He holds my hand,
With loving care;
And lets me know,
He's always there.

So, when my path,
I cannot see;
I squeeze His hand,
For He's guiding me.

And when this life,
For me is o'er;
I'll rest with Him,
On that distant shore.

I will not fear,
When death is mine;
For He has held my hand,
All this time.

09/26/2003 John 10:27

~ Steven R. Thacker ~

THE BLOOD THAT FELL AT CALVARY

The blood that fell at Calvary,
Was enough to set me free;
It flowed within my broken heart,
And showed my sin to me.

It stirred within this soul of mine,
A longing that was real;
Where now a peace resides within,
Before was cold as steel.

Calvary's blood has washed away,
The pain of useless schemes;
It searched each crevice of my mind,
And now they're but distant dreams.

Now I dream of how my life can count,
And prosper for my Lord;
I'll place myself in the hands of God,
And cleave to His holy Word.

I'll place His armor on my life,
And never shall turn 'round;
For in my past is pain and woe,
But with God sweet joy abounds.

So, the blood that fell at Calvary,
Will always mean to me;
Sweet love—and joy—and peace within,
And precious victory.

2001

~ Steven R. Thacker ~

HE TOOK THE STRIFE

Secure in Jesus,
Oh, what a thought!
All my sins,
To Him I brought.

The broken pieces,
Of my life;
With all the hurt,
And all the strife.

I now abide,
Within His care;
I rest in Him,
His love to share.

Now all my guilt,
And all its pain;
Is safely placed,
Beneath that crimson stain.

For in His blood,
He took that strife;
And gave to me,
A brand new life.

08/15/2006 Psalms 40:1

~ Steven R. Thacker ~

HELP ME LORD

Though all the world would hate you, Lord,
And curse Your holy name;
Help me God to find the strength,
To not repeat the same.

If the masses choose to mock you, Lord,
And spit upon your brow;
May I still choose to love them, Lord,
Much more than I do now.

I find no courage within my shell,
To fight this evil foe;
But in you, Lord, I find much more,
Then I could ever show.

So, help me, Lord, to chart my course,
Close by the crimson flow;
And help me, Lord, to love you more.
And to follow where You go.

01/03/1995

THIS FAMILY

Our children gave us joy,
All those years gone by;
Their wondrous glow in winter's snow,
And that twinkle in their eye.

02/16/2007

~ Steven R. Thacker ~

HIS GENTLE CARE

Drifting on a shifting sand,
I teeter to and fro;
It seems that all around is dark,
And I wonder where to go.

But there's a hand that I can hold,
When fear my way assail;
He keeps me quiet in the storm,
In His grace that will not fail.

So, blow ye winds and howl ye gale,
You no longer frighten me;
For since I found His gentle care,
I sail a quiet sea.

09/29/2006

~ Steven R. Thacker ~

MY FRIEND

I walked along the hills of God,
And knew His grace divine;
I heard His voice in the gentle breeze,
Sweet joy and peace was mine.

And then I felt temptations pull,
To lead me from His face;
Would I depart and walk in sin,
And ignore His wondrous grace?

No, I must fight temptations grasp,
And I must follow Him;
For in His love I can't deny,
That He's my dearest friend.

02/15/2007

BEAUTY

Beauty is not the outward view,
That shows upon ones face;
True beauty comes from deep within,
And is empowered by God's grace.

03/17/2007

WHEN THE SAVIOR IS NEAR

When the Savior is near,
There's no need to fear.

11/720/11 1 John 4:18

~ Steven R. Thacker ~

HIS GUIDANCE

I am the object of His love,
In His sweet and gentle care;
I know that all is peace within,
With His loving presence there.

I dare not trust within myself,
To wonder here below;
Without His hand to guide my steps,
And help my way to know.

So, with my Savior at my side,
We'll travel with delight;
Until one day with saints above,
I'll take my heavenly flight.

06/02/2008

TO WIN A SOUL

To win a soul to God above,
Is such a wondrous thing;
To show to them the grace of God,
And the peace it truly brings.

For when a soul has made its flight,
From Satan's cords and snares;
They'll find sweet love and joy abounds,
Within His gentle care.

2007 Proverbs 11:30 & Psalms 126:6

~ Steven R. Thacker ~

THAT CRIMSON TIDE

Many are the objects,
Unearthed by mankind;
Once thought to be buried forever,
Was there for man to find.

Those secrets that we've hidden away,
Are sure to come again;
Though hid away for none to view,
But, our Lord reveals all sin.

Yet there's a covering designed of God,
That truly covers like a flood;
It flowed from off a wooden cross,
It's our Savior's precious blood.

It melts away each fallen tear,
And covers all our sinful past;
The crimson tide of God's dear Son,
Will give hope and peace at last.

12/8/2009

COME

Come to God on bended knee,
And He'll make your life brand new;
The hurt and fear that you had borne,
He'll take away from you.

02/09/2007

~ Steven R. Thacker ~

WHERE'S THE BLAME?

When traveling through this world below,
We wonder why such grief;
Why is this world in such despair,
When God could bring relief?

Why do they strive to run a race,
That they could never win?
And why do they reject the Lord,
And choose to live in sin?

Well, we could blame the Devil,
With all his evil ways;
Or perhaps we point to fallen man,
And the part that Adam played.

No, we can't point to another,
To shoulder all the blame;
For when the roll is called above,
The Lord will call our name.

We're the one that must repent,
And fall on bended knee;
And we're the one that will feel the joy,
As He sets our spirits free.

So, don't accuse another,
For the shape this world is in;
Just step within the hand of God,
And place your faith in Him.

12/8/2009 II Corinthians 5:10

~ Steven R. Thacker ~

I MUST GO

The lost is all around me,
But I offer not a sound;
To tell them of the way to God,
So their salvation might be found.

I always fear the comment,
That they might offer me;
So, I just keep within my heart,
The hope that would set them free.

I wonder what the Lord would say,
When I before Him stand;
Will He agree with the choice I made,
Or point to that blood that's on my hands?

Can I ignore the call of God,
To witness as I go;
And tell them of a Savior's love,
So they might Heaven go?

Yes, I must speak with courage true,
And go where He would show;
To tell a lost and dying world,
Of a God who loves them so.

12/1995

JOY IN OUR JOURNEY

There is joy in the journey when Jesus is your guide.

11/22/11

~ Steven R. Thacker ~

I SEARCHED FOR PEACE

I once walked a lonely road,
That led me to despair;
I could not find the peace I sought,
Though I looked most everywhere.

I looked within great riches,
And the fame I might attain;
But it seemed that wherever I would search,
The answer was still the same.

But then one day I found it,
That peace I'd sought so long;
It wasn't in my crafty schemes,
For all my searching had been wrong.

On Calvary stood the answer,
Upon the cruel tree;
Sweet peace became my portion,
When Jesus set me free.

12/16/1995

WE STAND BEFORE OUR CHILDREN

We stand before our children,
And show both night and day;
They see us when we rightly live,
And when we go astray.

02/11/2001

~ Steven R. Thacker ~

I WONDER HOW

I wonder how the pills we take,
Each and every day;
Can know the route to travel,
Just how do they know the way?

Could there be a sign along inside,
That they could clearly see;
Or maybe there's a traffic cop,
Just who directs their way though me?

Those pills may help the headache,
And joints and backache too;
But truly all the healing comes,
From that One who died for you.

Now doctors have such training,
And their skill is known by men;
But without the hand of God on them,
They'd have no skills within.

For God's the Great Physician,
And He can touch your strife;
He'll calm the hurts and ease the pain,
And love you all through life.

So, don't worry over sickness,
And don't fret when pains arise;
Just trust the Lord to show the way,
For it's in Him the answers lie.

02/04/2007 Psalms 139:14

~ Steven R. Thacker ~

IN THE SHADOW

In the shadow of a cradle,
The Son of God was born;
Though poor and lowly was His birth,
With parents tired and worn.

The people of the town that day,
Could not behold the sight;
Those lowly Shepherds viewed with joy,
Of the Savior's birth that night.

The glory of a Holy God,
And the greatness of Heaven's throng;
The wonder of a parent's joy,
And the Angels and their song.

The King of kings in swaddling clothes,
In a dark and lowly stall;
Now comes to earth in the dead of night,
To give God's hope to all.

Yes, in the shadow of a cradle,
A baby strong and true;
And in the shadow of a cross,
He would die for me and you.

12/03/2006

HOPE RESTORED

When forgiveness is granted, hope is restored.

11/22/11

~ Steven R. Thacker ~

LABOR OF LOVE

Preach the Word,
Endure the test;
Remember that God,
Expects your best.

Redeem the time,
That the Lord has given you;
Instruct your people,
And help them through.

For the time may come,
When a lamb may fall;
And they turn to you,
And it's your name they call.

So, gather your strength,
From your Father above;
And remember your church,
Is a labor of love.

1996 To my fellow Pastors/Preachers/Ministers

EACH DAY

I rest each day in His loving arms,
And trust His guidance true;
For I know that whether life of death,
His grace will take me through.

05/04/2003

~ Steven R. Thacker ~

JOY

Joy will not come to us,
By things we may achieve;
With things we have within our homes,
Or the plans we may conceive.

The joy that man will often have,
Is empty and not enough;
It leaves him feeling incomplete,
When times get really rough.

The joy that comes from God above,
Is different in every way;
It gives you strength to carry on,
Through the darkness into day.

The joy that rests in God alone,
Is anchored deep and strong;
Not in the futile things we do,
But in Jesus where they belong.

09/2919/95

GOD'S GENTLE TOUCH

A gentle touch,
From God's sweet hand;
Will bring relief,
To a troubled land.

11/6/2011

"Pray for our Nation"

~ Steven R. Thacker ~

LETTING GO

Letting go of the pain within,
Is not an easy task;
It seems to fill my every thought,
Both now and from my past.

How can I free my troubled mind,
And set my spirit free;
How can I break these chains of hurt,
And find sweet peace for me?

I've found the answer within God's Word,
And it gives me hope again;
He says to give those hurts to Him,
And He'll take away the pain.

Though the answer seems too simple,
He says we can attain;
By taking hold of the Master's hand,
And letting go of the pain.

03/07/2007

ALL I NEED

All I need in thee I find,
Great peace and hope and love;
No greater friend can there be found,
Then my Savior from above.

2005

~ Steven R. Thacker ~

THE MAN OF GOD

The man of God must know God's will,
To feed the flock in love;
And he can't discern the will of God,
Unless it's from above.

The heart of man is hard to know,
Their needs you cannot see;
For only God can view the heart,
To set the captive free.

So, search His Word and know His will,
And share with them in love;
That message He has given you,
From His precious home above.

10/2006 A challenge to the Pastor

THE DAY WILL COME

The day will come,
When all will be peace;
With toils all gone,
And sacred songs release.

With battles all over,
And work all done;
We'll abide in the presence,
Of God's dear Son.

08/13/2011

~ Steven R. Thacker ~

TIME

Yesterday is a hurdle,
That can never be jumped again;
And tomorrow is a time,
Best left to the Master, my friend.

For worrying about tomorrow,
And grieving over the past;
Can only cause a burdened heart,
And a peace that will not last.

So, give to God tomorrow,
And trust Him for your past;
Then you will find the journey,
Will give joy and peace at last.

12/16/06

THE HANDS OF GOD

The hands of God,
Will dry your tears;
They'll give you peace,
And calm your fears.

When heartache causes,
Pain and grief;
Those hands of God,
Will bring relief.

2008

~ Steven R. Thacker ~

LORD, HELP ME SEE

Lord, help me see today,
What I truly am;
Have I the love to stand for Thee,
When judged by another man?

Have I the desire within my soul,
To serve Thee day by day?
Or will I be as others are,
And simply turn away?

When times of fear and doubt arise,
Will I yet stem the flood?
Or willing as the mighty have,
And give if need be my blood?

Have I the courage, Lord, to take,
Upon my human frame;
The cross of pain and bitter tears,
Or will I yet refrain?

When You would call for one to stand,
Upon the battle line;
May I be willing, Lord, to say,
"Take me, Lord, I am thine."

2002 Psalms 7:1

WHEN FAITH IS PRESENT

When faith is present then fear is absent.
11/22/11

~ Steven R. Thacker ~

MAKE EACH DAY COUNT

The years seem to pass us by,
As we consider life;
One day we're in a cradle small,
And the next we take a wife.

Our parents who are strong and true,
And present when tears fly;
Are all too soon turned old and gray,
And will lose their strength and die.

I find in life the desperate need,
To cling to life and pray;
For God to give a love for life,
And cherish each passing day.

The day may cloud and turn to rain,
But soon the sun has shown;
So, grasp with tender hands of love,
And make each day your own.

2003

SPIRITUAL INSIGHT

God through Christ hath set me free,
He paid my debt on Calvary;
I want to serve and more faithful be,
When I see Him on that cursed tree.

2010

~ Steven R. Thacker ~

MY STEADFAST ANCHOR

Many are the storms,
That batter every day;
The force at times,
Could make us stray.

But beneath our vessel,
One day was cast;
The anchor of God,
That always holds fast.

Though mighty would,
That tempest be;
My faithful God,
Holds tight to me.

So, let the tempest,
Come my way;
I know my Anchor,
Will always stay.

03/20/07 Psalms 121:1-2 & Psalms 3:3

THE SAVIOR IN FULL CONTROL

He's the giver of salvation,
And the keeper of my soul;
There can be no greater peace of mind,
Then the Savior in full control.

2009

~ Steven R. Thacker ~

OUR EVER PRESENT GUIDE

Though my foes may beset me,
Each way that I would go;
I reach forth in faith,
To the Savior I know.

Though the storms may be strong,
On each and every side;
I stay close to Jesus,
Where I safely abide.

Though we walk in the midst,
Of a crooked and perverse land;
Our anchor holds fast,
In the Master's strong hand.

09/02/90

A MOTHER'S PRAYER

A gentle touch and warm embrace,
Brings a smile to our Savior's face;
For tiny hands need loving care,
And the precious sound of a Mother's prayer.

2008

A PATTERN

What greater pattern, can we show;
That when heartache arises, it's to God we go?

11/6/2011

~ Steven R. Thacker ~

PRESS ON

The hand of God is always near,
To aid us in our work;
If we but ask and seek His face,
And not His children shirk.

For Jesus died for all of these,
The small as well as great;
He gives the measure of His grace,
To reach them before it's too late.

So, press on to the battle front,
And cast aside all doubt;
For we are on the winning side,
And we soon shall hear the shout.

01/24/98

THE BENDED KNEE

On bended knee,
Is a posture that's right;
As we address the One,
Who gives love and light.

PRAYER

God's guidance is there,
When we've knelt in prayer.

11/4/2011

~ Steven R. Thacker ~

MY PRAYER FOR YOU

May the Lord be swift to guide,
In the path you ought to tread;
And may your heart be always tender,
As you feed on the Living Bread.

The eyes of God are open,
When we search His will to find;
As we fret not of our human needs,
But strive for that spiritual kind.

So, keep your eyes upon the furrow,
And your hands upon the plow;
Though the way seem rough and rocky,
And sweat show on the brow.

Our Savior draws much closer,
To that child that's doing right;
Who is not afraid of the battle strong,
For his strength is in God's might.

12/.05/90 James 5:16

GOD'S CONTROL

A faithful life,
Should be our goal;
And it can only be found,
Within God's control.

02/19/07

~ Steven R. Thacker ~

PROPER THINKING

We dwell upon the numbers,
That once was gathered here;
And question what the problem is,
Is there ought that I should fear?

And then a calm assurance,
Fills my mind and soul;
It's not in me that growth occurs,
But the Lord who's in control.

May I be guilty of one thing,
That truly is my part;
And this is one of loving,
Much more than from the start.

For if my crime be loving,
The sheep of God's own heart;
Then He will fill this building,
With those who'll do their part.

2005 I Corinthians 3:7

MY STEPS

My steps will be on golden streets,
And my eyes will be on heavenly joys;
My heart will rejoice in the presence of God,
And the hurts of life will no longer annoy.

01/01/07

~ Steven R. Thacker ~

THE GRUMP STUMP

One day as I was walking,
Down a familiar lane;
I heard someone complaining,
About how certain things were lame.

It caused me to consider,
The things I gripe about;
And how I must grieve my Lord,
When He sees me moan and pout.

I thought about the damage.
When I grump in public view;
And others see my discontent,
And not a servant true.

So, I spoke to one dear brother,
Who cut for me a stump;
So I may climb upon it,
And in private be a grump.

Now in the seclusion of my home,
When I feel the need to grump;
I simply go into my bedroom,
And climb upon my stump.

9/21/1994 Psalms 100:1-2

To my friend Roger Davis, Blessed Hope Baptist Church, Spgfld, OH

~ Steven R. Thacker ~

THE MANY

Many are the heartaches,
That comes to mortal man;
And many are the challenges,
That's found throughout the land.

Many are the heroes,
With courage for the fight;
And many are the home fires,
That watches both day and night.

Many are the preachers,
Who stand alone for God;
And many were the martyrs,
Whose blood spilled on the sod.

Too often we will notice those,
Whose shame has caused us grief;
And overlook the many,
Who bring such sweet relief.

01/23/2007 II Tim. 4:7-8

~ Steven R. Thacker ~

NOT BY WORKS ALONE

Man may try to find a way,
To reach sweet Heaven's shore;
By the deeds they've done,
Or by the works they've laid in store.

But when we stand before God's throne,
With all we have achieved;
We'll find that nothing we have done,
Will eternal life receive.

For nothing short of God's own Son,
And the blood from Calvary's tree;
Will purchase one from Satan's grasp,
And the soul from sin set free.

So, trust not in the things you've done,
And the works of life alone;
To satisfy a Holy God,
And your sinful lives atone.

For life with God is not to be,
Through the deeds of mortal man;
For God in mercy before time began,
Devised Salvation's plan.

03/16/1996

TIME

Time is a treasurer that can only be spent once.

11/22/11

~ Steven R. Thacker ~

O THE JOY

O the joy that comes to me,
When serving with my Lord;
I could not wish a greater lot,
Then my Savior's sweet accord.

He lifts when I feel weary,
And He comforts when I'm sad;
He truly is the greatest friend,
This traveler has ever had.

He never leaves me lonely,
Though friends my leave my side;
He's always there to cheer me on,
An ever present guide.

Though deep may be my valley,
And rough may be the gale;
I know with God to guide me,
I truly shall prevail.

So, thank you, Lord, for giving joy,
Each step of every day;
It gives me courage to go on,
I'll trust you all the way.

For I have learned to listen, Lord,
Since the day you set me free;
There's no problem that I can't face,
As long as you're with me.

09/30/1995

~ Steven R. Thacker ~

SAFE IN THE MASTER'S HAND

If the path that lies before us,
Was mapped by God's own hand;
We need not fear when tempest blows,
Though the earth seem as sinking sand.

Though all that would oppress us,
In storm or weather fair;
It's not for us to fret about,
When we're in the Master's care.

So, set your course on things above,
And point your compass true;
Though wind and storm beset your craft,
He'll gently guide you through.

There is no fear this world could give,
As I travel through this land;
When my faith is placed in Jesus Christ,
I'm safe in the Master's hand.

11/23/1994 Psalms 91:1

FLOWERS

Flowers from the garden,
Can help us when we're down;
But flowers only encourage the living,
And not when we're no longer around.

11/31/11

~ Steven R. Thacker ~

SERVING

I want to serve my Lord,
Not because of men;
And the credit I might attain,
But because it pleases Him.

I want to walk within His path,
Because I know it's right;
Not because of foolish pride,
Or fears that come at night.

Serving God is joy and peace,
To one who knows God's will;
That one that serves in spite of pain,
His wondrous plan fulfills.

They know that nothing that life affords,
Should take their Savior's place;
They serve Him because they love Him,
And because of His amazing grace.

1994 Deuteronomy 10:12

~ Steven R. Thacker ~

LEND A HAND

Lend a hand, my brother,
And help them in their need;
For God will bless your efforts true,
As you plant that loving seed.

11/31/11

SPEAK UP CHRISTIAN

How great the cause of Christ would spread,
If Believers would only say;
Of all the Lord hath done for them,
And the shackles He's taken away.

How far the Gospel story would go,
And no one could ever tell;
Of how many souls would turn to God,
And alter their course from Hell.

So, speak the things that God hath done,
To give you peace within;
Who paid that price untold for you,
To free your soul from sin.

2009

~ Steven R. Thacker ~

THE SHADOW OF THE CROSS

In the shadow of the cross,
The heart is made brand new;
It removes a life of sin and shame,
And pain and hatred too.

It's now a place of inner joy,
Where love and peace abides;
Where once all hope had gone away,
God's grace is now inside.

The shadow of that wooden cross,
Where Jesus bled for me;
Is now a place where my blessed Lord,
Has set my spirit free.

10/15/2006

~ Steven R. Thacker ~

GOD'S OWN SON

The day will come,
When all is peace;
With toils all gone,
And sacred songs release.

The battle will be over,
And the victory will be won;
As we joy in the presence,
Of the Father's own dear Son.

06/2011

TELL THE LOST

Bring the lost to Jesus, friend,
If they with hope would be;
For they are held in Satan's grasp,
And they must be set free.

The task is not an easy one,
To tell to sinful man;
That Jesus died for all the world,
As His Blood fell on the sand.

But we must bear within our minds,
That Hell awaits the lost;
So, press the message to all men,
That Jesus paid the cost.

02/05/1989

~ Steven R. Thacker ~

BE A WITNESS

The souls of man are in danger,
And needs a witness true;
We can't relinquish to another's hand,
What God has called us to do.
11/6/2011

TRUST

Trust in God, and faith in Him;
Will free a life, that's been bound by sin.
11/8/2011

THE CHOICES THAT WE MAKE

There are choices made within this life,
That all around we see;
They may affect those that we love,
Or alter what may be.

But the choice we make with Jesus,
Is one we make alone;
And though we may think it matters not,
It will one day be placed in stone.

So, trust the Lord and live for Him.
A life that's true and brave;
For joy will come at daybreak,
In that life beyond the grave.
11/10/2004

CHOICES

One may choose popularity,
And the accolades of men;
While some may choose possessions,
To comfort their every whim.

Yet those who choose the Savior,
And a path of truth and right;
Will one day soar with eagles,
In that land where God's Son is the light.
11/7/2011

~ Steven R. Thacker ~

TEARS

We shed a tear when someone dies,
We shed a tear when a baby is born;
We shed a tear for a beautiful sky,
We shed a tear when a brother's torn.

We shed a tear when a song hits home,
We shed a tear when our youngest is wed;
We shed a tear when our team has won,
We shed a tear for the martyred dead.

But will we shed a tear,
And do we care for the lost in sin;
When they die without knowing God,
And go to a Hell that's without end?

Oh, yes, I must be willing,
To bravely speak my case;
Of how Jesus gave His precious blood,
For the entire human race.

2007 Psalms 126:5-6

COMFORT

When your heart is burdened,
And you find no peace within;
Just turn that heart to Jesus,
For He's your dearest friend.

11/7/2011

~ Steven R. Thacker ~

WHEN DEATH IS MINE

When my eyes close in death,
There is one thing that I know;
They will open once again,
In the wonder of Heaven's glow.

In that land with heartaches gone,
And with sorrows left behind;
For all the joys of God's sweet grace,
In Heaven will be mine.

For all my loved ones who've gone before,
Will greet me on that strand;
O' the joy that awaits me,
In the midst of God's own hand.
09/24/2005

THE SHEDDING OF TEARS

When tears have stained our pillow,
And fear has filled our nights;
When all we've tried has failed us,
And our heart has lost its fight.

Then lift your heart to Jesus,
He's waiting for your call;
Then you will find the peace you need,
When you give to Him your all.
11/7/2011

~ Steven R. Thacker ~

THE BURDEN

The painful past,
Will quickly fade;
When taken to the Cross,
And then tenderly laid.

The burden of that heavy load,
Will ease beyond compare;
When the Savior takes those burdens,
And all those troubles and cares.

The problem is not in that load,
That weighs upon ones back;
It's really in all those senseless cares,
We think we have to pack.

It's not in the burdens,
That causes us such grief;
It's in that stubborn pride of self,
When we refuse God's sweet relief.

So, when the burden weighs you down,
And you begin to fall;
Just remember that God in love,
Has promised to take them all.

03/09/2007 Matthew 11:28-30

~ Steven R. Thacker ~

THE OFFERED LIFE

We offer God a life that's gone,
All value left behind;
We have no gift to give to Him,
Just a worthless and empty kind.

We would not take the hand of God,
Through the Spirits constant plea;
The only friend we cared about,
Was I, myself, and me.

But now that death is at my door,
I seek God's loving care;
And hope that He will rescue me,
For now His love I'll share.

But why should God descend to me,
Upon my bed of woe;
When I rejected Him for years,
With a cruel and heartless, no?

You see He only comes to us,
Through repentance strong and true;
And then He takes us by the hand,
And will gently lead us through.

08/01/04 Psalms 89:15

~ Steven R. Thacker ~

THE PATH WE TAKE

The path we take each day we live,
Too often brings us pain;
As we choose with selfish plans in mind,
A course of personal gain.

We fail to see that God in love,
Has a plan for all we do;
He knows and wants the best for us,
And the goals we <u>should pursue</u>.

God wants to help and guide each day,
If we'd only take His hand;
And let Him lead each step we take,
Through this dark and troubled land.

So, take the time, dear child of God,
And trust His leading care;
You'll find though even dark the trail,
That God will meet you there.

05/03/200 To my co-laborer in Christ, William Brown, Jeremiah 15:16

GOD'S PATH

God leads in ways of peace and grace,
His compass ever true;
No matter what the burdens would be,
He'll take good care of you.

11/8/2011

~ Steven R. Thacker ~

THE RACE

The race is set before us,
And the course is hard to see;
We know not where this path may lead,
Over smooth or troubled seas.

We need only know the Master,
Has marked the way to take;
And as long as I would follow Him,
He shelters for my sake.

I know the trail is rocky,
And steep may be the climb;
But I sense the presence of my Lord,
Who walks with me all the time.

So, when my feet get weary,
And the finish lies before;
I'll hold tight to the Master's hand,
And pass on through Heaven's door.

07/19/1995 II Timothy 4:7-8

HE'S THERE

The One who raised up Lazarus,
And walked upon the sea;
Will chart my course each day I live,
And give sweet victory.

11/7/2011

~ Steven R. Thacker ~

THE ROAD OF LIFE

The road of life,
Is often steep;
There are curves ahead,
And valley's deep.

But those who travel,
Along this way;
Must stay on course,
And never stray.

For when we depart,
This road of life;
We'll find the way,
Is a path of strife.

But when the darkness,
Obscures the view;
We'll need to find,
A compass that's true.

God's own Word,
Will lead the way;
When Satan would tempt,
Our feet to stray.

So, hold God's hand,
And trust His might;
As on you travel,
This road of life.

03/20/2007 Psalms 91:2

~ Steven R. Thacker ~

THE SAILOR

How often would this sailor see,
Those storms in life that buffet me.

I try to hold with all my might,
But soon I see I've lost the fight.

How often God has whispered true,
"I'll lead your ship and abide with you."

So, help me, Lord, to construct my life,
To trust Your grace to calm my strife.

I'll hold real tight to that nail pierced hand,
And walk within your mighty plan.

For You can view that troubled sea,
And all those storms ahead of me.

So, courage, dear Lord, I need from you,
To safely guide this sailor through.

03/22/2007 Nahum 1:3

SAILING

All the storms that threaten our ship,
With all their trouble and strife;
Will fail in their efforts to conquer us,
With Jesus in our life.

11/6/2011

~ Steven R. Thacker ~

THIS CAPTIVE

I found one day my life was bound,
With fetters from my past;
I tried to gain release from them,
But they held me O' so fast.

I found no help for this my fate,
As I struggled to and fro;
Man's only council for my lot,
Was that I would more courage show.

Then one day God's precious peace,
Came to me strong and true;
"Your worth is much, dear child of mine,
For you see I died for you."

So, now I worry not my friend,
How man might council me;
For you see God came to earth one day,
To set this captive free.
01/1996 Romans 10:9-10

THE PRISONER

I was kept in prison strong,
And a jailer held the key;
Then Jesus paid the ransom price,
And set this prisoner free.
11/6/2011

~ Steven R. Thacker ~

TO ALL WHO BELIEVE

God gave the gift that the world would reject,
Jesus paid the price that mankind would not accept.

Though blood was spilled from a sinless side,
They turned away in foolish pride.

That scene from Calvary can be seen today,
In the resentful laughs and the things we say.

We reject the Christ who died for all,
And follow the steps of our parent's fall.

For you see in Eden the same was the case,
They rejected God's plan and sin entered the human race.

So, trust in Christ, His plan to receive,
For salvation is promised to all who believe.
04/9/1991

REDEMPTION'S PLAN

Redemption's plan was sealed of God,
Before the world began;
The cost was paid by His own Son,
And not through the schemes of man.
11/6/2011

~ Steven R. Thacker ~

TRUST HIM FOR THE PAST

The Lord alone can sooth my hurt,
That haunts me from my past;
He cares for me and helps me see,
His love is what will last.

He shows to me that all before,
Is covered by His blood;
And all I need is faith in Him,
To calm the whelming flood.

So, I know my Savior walks with me,
As I trust Him every day;
He leads me with His nail pierced hand,
And guides me all the way.

07/10/2004

TRUSTING GOD

If I can trust God for salvation,
And that home prepared above;
Then why not trust Him for the days ahead,
Protected by His love?

If He can feed the sparrow,
And care for the lilies in the field;
Then I know that He can shield my life,
As I would faithfully yield.

11/6/2011

~ Steven R. Thacker ~

TO MARK A PASSING

We come to mark a passing,
In this place we hold so dear;
A place that God has smiled upon,
For all these fifty years.

A church is more than mortar,
And the trim that lines the halls;
It's more than just a pulpit,
And a verse upon the wall.

The church is not the building,
It's the people that serve inside;
It takes a heart and gentle soul,
For God's blessings to abide.

So many souls have come and gone,
Since the day you first began;
But each was needed and had a part,
In the Master's wondrous plan.

So, we mark this day for God,
And the years that's come and gone;
Let's not forget those loving souls,
That came and stood so strong.

May God's sweet grace help us stand,
And hold His banner true;
Let's not retreat from serving God,
Until the battle's through.

10/2002 for the 50th Anniversary—Liberty Baptist Church—Pueblo, CO.

~ Steven R. Thacker ~

TRUSTING GOD

I trust the Lord when the sky is blue,
And joy is all around;
It isn't hard to walk with God,
When sadness can't be found.

There's always a smile upon my face,
When the days are bright and clear;
I have the faith to face the foe,
When my heart is free from fear.

But when the clouds of discontent,
Around my vessel lie;
I fold my hands and plead to God,
"Please help me lest I die."

The hand of God then calms my heart,
As He moves those clouds away;
He gives to me sweet joy and peace,
And strength for another day.

03/21/1996 Proverbs 3:5-7

TRUSTING

Trusting is not seen by what we say,
When all is going right;
Real trust is seen in what we do,
As we stand within God's might.

11/6/2011

~ Steven R. Thacker ~

HE'S ALWAYS THERE

When walking in this world below,
Our feet will often slide;
But we can face the rocky climb,
With Jesus at our side.

Today we're in a valley low,
With darkness all around;
But soon the dawn will break for us,
And we'll be Heaven bound.

So, let the raging tempest blow,
And see each battle through;
For there's one thing, dear child of God,
Your Lord will walk with you.

He takes us gently by the hand,
And never leaves our side;
And we can safely stay on course,
With Jesus as our guide.

So, keep your faith in God alone,
And take each step with prayer;
For He will safely see you through,
Because He's always there.

12/1996 Psalms 23:4

~ Steven R. Thacker ~

HEROES

Many are the heroes,
That passes us every day;
They show their love and kindness,
In a hundred different ways.

They come from all around us,
Throughout this land so grand;
They seek not for the applause of men,
But to hold a hurting hand.

True heroes have no color,
Nor creed or race to claim;
They only want to ease some pain,
Of the crippled, blind or lame.

A hero won't seek glory,
From the one that would applaud;
They only turn with humbled heart,
To give glory back to God.

For they know of just one Hero,
Who deserves our faithful praise;
He's the One who healed the blind man,
And caused the dead to raise.

He only deserves our worship,
And then it will be true;
That as we give Him the glory,
He'll make heroes out of you.

12/7/2009

~ Steven R. Thacker ~

WHAT IF JESUS CALLED ME HOME?

If Jesus viewed my wasted life,
Would there be teardrops fall?
Could He accept my empty tries,
To follow at His call?

Should I be fearful at that day,
When I before Him stand?
Will all my works be solid gold,
Or burnt cinders on the sand?

What would the sentence be for me,
If God would call me home?
As I would stand before His throne,
And stand there all alone.

Please help me, Lord, today to see,
The man I <u>need</u> to be;
And serve You with a heart that's true,
And be a faithful man for Thee.

So, when I stand before Thy throne,
And see Your wondrous face;
May I be known as a soldier true,
And not stand in sad disgrace.

01/13/2005

WHEN JESUS CALLS

When Jesus calls we should never put Him on hold.

11/22/11

~ Steven R. Thacker ~

UNCHANGING ONE

When grief upon my heart doth soar,
And terror buffets me;
I hold to Thee unchanging one,
And soon my heartaches flee.

When flames across my life doth spread,
And causes loss to me;
I hold to Thee unchanging one,
And fears won't present be.

When something takes from my life,
And breath is gone from me;
I'll hold to Thee unchanging one,
For Your face I soon will see.

It matters not what life would send,
For Your peace You gave to me;
And I'll hold to Thee unchanging one,
For Your grace hath set me free.

10/18/2007

GOD IS CONSTANT

We waver when we're buffeted,
In our ship so small and frail;
But the constant God who holds our life,
Will never ever fail.

11/5/2011

~ Steven R. Thacker ~

WHEN HEAVEN CHIMES

I cross through darkness from this life,
To a land of great release;
My mortal frame removed from earth,
To a land of perfect peace.

I leave behind me loved ones dear,
Who shared with me my load;
And though they shed a tear down here,
I marvel in God's abode.

If I could send but one regret,
To you I love so dear;
I think that it would be your hurt,
Of all those fallen tears.

But weep not over the joys we've had,
And the friendship that we've known;
For all these things will be enhanced,
Around our Father's throne.

Remember that our parting,
Is only for a time;
For our hearts and lives will meet again,
When the cords of Heaven chime.

So, keep in mind, dear friends of mine,
When your hearts give out a sigh;
That when the trumpet sounds above,
I'll meet you in the sky.

2008

~ Steven R. Thacker ~

WHEN THE MASTER BUILDS A LIFE

The Christian life is not to be,
A label on ones clothes;
It's not the suit or dress you wear,
Or the rules you would impose.

The proper walk with Jesus,
Is started from within;
We offer up our lives to God,
Through repentance He frees from sin.

From this a seed begins to grow,
To change our total man;
Our hopes, our dreams, our every sigh,
Are now part of the Master's plan.

He takes our weak and feeble frame,
And fashions with such care;
That when the world would look at us,
They'd see the Savior there.

So, build your life upon the Lord,
And let Him work through you;
You'll have a life with God's sweet peace,
When the Master's work is through.

1994

THE CARPENTER

When Jesus builds a life, it will stand all storms of strife.
11/22/11

~ Steven R. Thacker ~

WHY?

Why stumble in the darkness,
When the light of God is near?
And why fret over sadness,
When He has promised to dry each tear?

Why walk in constant worry,
And live in constant dread?
When Jesus in His abiding love,
Has promised He's the living bread?

He walked with Paul and Silas,
He healed the blind man too;
And He will not forsake His child,
For He'll always stay close by you.

01/26/2007

WHEN DARKNESS OBSCURES

When darkness obscures,
The truth and the way;
I call on the One,
Who turns darkness to day.

His Word is so clear,
And His guidance so right;
I no longer will fear,
The terror of night.

11/6/2011

~ Steven R. Thacker ~

BE A VOLUNTEER

Volunteers are needed,
As we walk this world below;
The land in which we find ourselves,
Is lost in sin and woe.

They need to see the Savior,
In our daily walk and life;
They need to see that there is hope,
For peace in a world of strife.

But if the work of Jesus,
Is left undone and still;
How will they find their way to God?
And who will show to them His will?

Yes, volunteers are needed,
Will you give to Him your love?
And let the Master fashion your life,
To the Savior's plans above?

03/24/2002

GOD'S CALL

God has called us,
To watch and to pray;
And soon the day will dawn,
As He rolls those clouds away.

11/6/2011

~ Steven R. Thacker ~

CALVARY'S BLOOD

The blood that fell at Calvary,
Was enough to cleanse from strife;
It broke those chains that held me fast,
And gave to me new life.

The blood that fell at Calvary,
Was enough to conquer sin;
It covered all the guilt in me,
And placed sweet peace within.

Yes, that blood that fell at Calvary,
Was enough to set me free;
And I'll never cease to praise my Lord,
For that blood from Calvary.

12/2007 Hebrews 9:22

THE TREE

God has sent His Son,
To die for you and me;
As He paid my sin,
Upon that tree.

All the shame,
That should have been mine;
Was placed on Him,
For all mankind.

11/6/2011

~ Steven R. Thacker ~

WHAT WOULD GOD SAY?

We shall hear from God above,
When life is at an end;
"A welcome home, you faithful one,"
From our closest and dearest friend.

The One with scars upon His hands,
And the ones upon His feet;
Will gently take us by the hand,
And lead through Heaven's streets.

So, worry not for battles here,
And the cares throughout the day;
For it matters not what man may do,
But only what God would say.
04/02/2005

IF

If I were afforded,
To save all men;
To offer them Heaven,
And their soul to win.

Would I be willing,
As God has shown;
To save the world,
Through a son of my own?
11/6/2011

~ Steven R. Thacker ~

DOES IT MATTER?

Does it matter if the life I live,
Is occupied by sin?
Does it matter if the things I do,
Involves me with evil men?

Does it matter if I neglect the ones,
That God has given me?
Does it matter if I turn away,
From the One who set me free?

Yes, it matters when I break the heart,
Of the loved ones in my life;
And it matters when I choose a course,
That deserts a path that's right.

It matters to my Savior,
Who died on Calvary;
And when I think of the price He paid,
It should really matter to me.

We need to think back at times,
To that cruel and bloody tree;
And recall the price that Jesus paid,
As He died to set us free.

02/10/2007 Psalms 37:23-24

IT MATTERS

The footprints left behind will be there for others to find.

11/22/11

~ Steven R. Thacker ~

DON'T QUIT

In times when trouble fills my life,
I find I want to stray;
When all the world seems upside down,
And I want to run away.

It's then I find no strength in me,
And I simply want to leave;
It seems no progress can be found,
And I only want to grieve.

It's then I think of Calvary,
And the hill He had to climb;
As walking toward that wooden cross,
And that pain that should have been mine.

He didn't slow His progress,
Though the crowd would see Him fall;
With bloody back and a crown of thorns,
He determined to give His all.

So, in my mind when I view that scene,
And the angry crowd that day;
My troubles and my sorrows,
Just seem to melt away.

How can I quit on Jesus,
When I view that bloody tree;
And I think of my dear Savior,
Who wouldn't quit on me?

02/10/2007

~ Steven R. Thacker ~

EVERY TIME

When walking through the valley,
And dark may be my trail;
I keep my eyes on Thee, my God,
The One who never fails.

The shadows may confuse my path,
Still onward I must tread;
For I am sure that it won't long,
'Til I see that Living Bread.

But when weary are the steps I take,
And rough may be the climb;
My hope is in the Lord above,
Who helps me every time.

2004

WHEN YOU ARE TROUBLED

When you are troubled about tomorrow,
And you seek some comfort true;
Remember that God has called you near,
To love and care for you.

He's there in the darkness,
When comfort cannot be found;
And He's there in the valley,
So, just stop and look around.

11/31/11

~ Steven R. Thacker ~

A VIEW OF THE GARDEN

I heard a voice so tender,
One night in darkness pray;
He spoke with such compassion,
I'll not forget that day.

He said, "Father, if Thou be willing,
Remove this cup from me;
Nevertheless, not my will,
But Thine be done," He said so free.

Then I realized so clearly,
Who knelt in front of me;
It was the Savior of the world,
Who would set the captives free.

So, I knelt and sought forgiveness,
Of those sins within my life;
And as I lifted up my head in prayer,
My soul had taken flight.

No longer was I a prisoner,
Bound by sin and woe;
My life is now worth living,
As I use His strength to go.

I'm so glad I went to the garden,
And viewed the Savior there;
For my life now has a purpose,
As I want His Word to share.

2/6/2004

~ Steven R. Thacker ~

REMIND ME LORD

Remind me Lord,
So that I might see;
Many of my loved ones,
Faithfully trust in thee.

For the locked door of my heart,
Must take a special key;
Please change my life,
So you can use me.

Help me to know,
Dear Savior of mine;
That without being saved,
They'll be left behind.

So, revive me, Lord,
And make me new;
That I might be a witness,
And be used by you.
11/05/1995

KNEEL AND PRAY

When troubles seek to hurt you,
And the tempter shows his face;
Just kneel and pray, dear child of God,
And seek God's loving grace.
11/31/11

~ Steven R. Thacker ~

THOSE HANDS

Those hands that fashioned,
The rolling sea;
Can surely be trusted,
To care for me.

Those hands that caress,
The trembling heart;
Will guide me through death,
When it's my time to part.

And those hands that led me,
All the days of my life;
Will lead me safely,
To His home so bright.

So when I have fear,
About the end of life;
I'll recall those hands,
That I've held so tight.

06/27/2008

THE HAND OF GOD

The hand of God will guide you,
In the day and in the night;
It matters not what the enemy does,
Just squeeze His hand real tight.

11/31/11

~ Steven R. Thacker ~

WHAT IF?

What if there was no Heaven?
And what if there was no Hell?
What if there were no mansions,
For saints one day to dwell?

What if there was no eternity,
Beyond this world below?
And what if this life was all there was,
With no hope beyond to know?

Then I would not want life to alter,
From the one I lived below;
For the friends I have are precious,
With no greater love to show.

For Church and Christ and Bible,
Have made my life so sweet;
And what if there was no Heaven,
I could not be more complete.

But there is indeed a Heaven,
And a life beyond the blue;
In that wondrous place awaiting,
That God has fashioned for you.

For in God's Book tis' written,
The facts for all to see;
For there's a place for all redeemed,
Where my loved ones wait for me.

08/13/2011 John 14:1-3

~ Steven R. Thacker ~

THE MIGHTY OAK

The mighty oak stands so tall,
Upon the mountain free;
Its lofty height and branches seen,
As it waves in summers breeze.

Few will doubt the strength of it,
Through storms and winds and hail;
While all around the timbers fall,
Yet the mighty oak prevails.

But if the oak could speak to you,
He would make the matter known;
While eyes are on his mighty frame,
The strength is where he's grown.

So, it's not the tall and lofty height,
That reaches up toward God;
It's the roots that lie beneath that tree,
Down deep within the sod.

We are like the oak tree,
With strength for all to see;
But it's not within our human frame,
It's those roots beneath our tree.

2005

GOD LEADS

God leads each day with His loving care,
His grace and peace is always there.

11/3/2011

~ Steven R. Thacker ~

SECTION 3

**Memorial poems for those
who were special to me.**

OUR FOOTPRINTS

Troublesome days,
May fill our life;
Both sickness and pain,
And sometimes strife.

But friends and loved ones,
Can ease the grief;
And a loving word,
Can bring relief.

This booklet is filled,
With some of these;
Who were kind and true,
Like a gentle breeze.

They would hold your hand,
And lift your load;
But now they've gone,
To Heaven's abode.

But their footprints are here,
And their witness is true;
To help us in hard times,
And to make our way through.

May we strive as they did,
To live our life below;
And leave the right footprints,
And a godly path show.

For one day soon,
When our journey is done;
We'll need to give an answer,
To God's dear Son.

09/15/2009

~ Steven R. Thacker ~

A SEASON OF TIME

Too often time has passed us,
As its seasons come and go;
And we marvel at the beauty,
Of a winter's falling snow.

Now we have a season,
That comes to one and all;
As we travel through our constant change,
And wait for God's sweet call.

David loved his family,
And he prayed for them I know;
He loved his wife of many years,
For this would truly show.

But now his chair is empty,
About the table scene;
And his voice will now be silent,
Where his laughter once had been.

But in the courts of glory,
Where Jesus stands nearby;
David fills another seat,
And he waits with a tender sigh.

For now our hearts are burdened,
And our tears will freely fall;
Until that day when we will hear,
Our Savior's loving call.

So, grieve not for his passing,
For now he walks above;
He's greeting all who've gone before,
And he's resting in God's love.

06/24/2008 In memory of David Dillard—Blessed Hope Baptist, Spgfld, OH

~ Steven R. Thacker ~

WHEN WALKING ON THE MOUNTAIN TOP

When walking on the mountain top,
It's easy to praise the Lord;
To thank Him for His blessed peace,
And our Savior's sweet accord.

It's easy to say, "I love you, Lord,"
When things are going right;
When we feel so very close to God,
In the day and in the night.

I feel that when we please our Lord,
Is in the valley low;
When all of life is dark and drear,
And we use His strength to go.

So, praise the Lord with all your heart,
Whether valley or mountain high;
And place your life in the Master's hands,
And lift your faith to the sky.

1978 Isaiah 40:31

In Memory of Sis. Grim, one of my Jolly 60's, Bible Baptist Church, Xenia, Ohio

~ Steven R. Thacker ~

A TRIBUTE TO SHERRY WISEMAN

She walked with God and loved her mate,
And raised her children three;
She loved her church and the Word of God,
A testimony to you and me.
There seemed to be a special bond,
Between Sherry and her Jim;
He was not just her loving mate,
But was her dearest friend.

She had so many storms in health,
That caused her body grief;
But now she walks with God on high,
Her soul has found relief.
We know that Jim and their children too,
Will grieve for her this day;
I know many will ask with tears,
Why God took her away.

We wonder why such passings are,
With people such as she;
But there is no greater place,
Then at her Savior's knee.
Now rest assured, dear grieving souls,
There is hope for you today;
For Sherry now rests with her Lord,
And it's there she wants to stay.

The greatest honor that we could give,
To Sherry on this day;
Is for you to trust in God alone,
For He is the only way.
He is the Way, the Truth, the Life,
For hope beyond this day;
So, trust Him, serve Him and love Him,
Make Him your hope and stay.

06/07/2001 In Memory of Sherry Wiseman, Freedom Baptist Temple, Xenia, Oh

~ Steven R. Thacker ~

AT PEACE WITH HIM

The body that's laid before you here,
Is one of peace and rest;
She lived a life of inner strength,
And gave to God her best.

She always saw the best in man,
No matter how rough the trail;
For in her heart she knew her Lord,
Was one who would never fail.

There are so often too few we find,
Of those who truly share;
Who walk with God each day they live,
And show the world they care.

Dear June, we thank the Lord so true,
Who held you in His love;
That you are now at peace with Him,
In that wondrous home above.

05/19/2005 In memory of June Dean—Liberty Baptist, Pueblo. CO.

~ Steven R. Thacker ~

AT TIMES WE WONDER

Vivian walked with God above,
And knew His blessed Word;
Her mind was sharp and knew His will,
And her salvation was secured.

For in His hands she had placed her life,
So many years ago;
And wished to truly walk with Him,
And all His wonders know.

The stages of her life it seems,
Had taken such a turn;
The mind that once was quick and sharp,
Now was hidden and caused concern.

Her journey now has led her,
To that land beyond compare;
Where life's confusions are left behind,
And she rests in her Savior's care.

The loved ones that have gone before,
Are now within her view;
And she prays that one sweet day,
You'll trust her Savior too.

05/30/2006 in Memory of Vivian McClure, Liberty Baptist Church, Pueblo, CO.

~ Steven R. Thacker ~

CORA "GRANDMA WEAVER"

To those who gather here to mourn,
In this place today;
You may want to take some time to think,
Or the honor you wish to pay.

As your thoughts return to yesteryear,
And some treasurers come to mind;
To see this precious one again,
And that face that seemed to shine.

This casket made by mortal hands,
And fashioned with such care;
Encases just an earthly shell,
For her spirit is now elsewhere.

We merely pay respect today,
Of this one who walked with God;
For now this precious saint's above,
Her feet on Heaven's sod.

The tears that fall from eyes today,
Fall only for our sorrow;
For this world will feel the space,
Of no Cora here tomorrow.

Cora was a shining star,
For many here today;
She always had much love to give,
Much more than we could say.

~ Steven R. Thacker ~

I have much peace within my heart,
As I rest with comforts thought;
That Grandma rests in the arms of Christ,
In the presence of almighty God.

Her journey here on earth is through,
But her life with God has just begun;
Her trials and pains down here are gone,
She's now with God's dear Son.

If she were here to speak to you,
I know what she might say;
"I'm not in pain, but only joy,
And this I want for you today.

But this only comes through faith in Christ,
And no other way will do;
Just trust Him as your Lord and Savior,
And someday you'll be here too."
11/1990 In memory of Cora Weaver, My Grandma

MY GRANDMA

She always stood for Jesus,
And was often heard to say;
I'll trust Him in the darkness,
And in the light of day.
11/31/11

~ Steven R. Thacker ~

HE WALKED IN GENTLE KINDNESS

He walked in gentle kindness,
With a smile upon his face;
I found in him a loving friend,
And no one could take his place.

I loved to be around him,
To feel his joy and grace;
It seemed no matter what his pain,
He gave a warm embrace.

There were times I tried to offer,
Some comfort to impart;
But when I left this gentle man,
It was I who with peace would part.

I know that there will be many,
Lonely days ahead;
Of memories of those days gone by,
And they'll be tears that we will shed.

But we must think beyond this day,
And place them in God's care;
As he goes to that land of God,
With beauty beyond compare.

I do not know what tomorrow holds,
The day is not yet past;
But when we move to realms above,
We'll meet again at last.

11/17/2006 In Memory of Max Fries, Liberty Baptist Church, Pueblo, CO

~ Steven R. Thacker ~

HE WALKED IN GENTLE PEACE

He walked in gentle peace,
A caring and loving man;
He cared more about others than himself,
To lend a helping hand.

He didn't like to dwell on self,
And to complain about the day;
He would rather think of better times,
When the family would laugh and play.

Lester was always a joy to see,
And pleasant to be around;
He liked to show a smiling face,
And seldom would wear a frown.

His presence will be sadly missed,
As we move from day to day;
But the joy and love that he left behind,
Will comfort us along our way.

This gentle man has gone to God,
And now abides above;
He now unites with loved ones dear,
Embraced in our Savior's love.

05/18/2003 In Memory of Lester Pruitt, Victory Baptist Church, Jamestown, OH

SWEET PEACE

Sweet peace would be our portion, if the Lord would have our devotion.

11/27/11

~ Steven R. Thacker ~

HER LIFE

Her life was one of laughter,
Her presence filled the room;
She never would be satisfied,
With a life that was filled with gloom.

She loved to watch the excitement,
Upon the children's face;
She gave to them the Word of God,
And shared with them His grace.

She loved the young and old alike,
And prayed for them each day;
She tried to give them strength and hope,
To chase their hurt away.

She had a special love and grace,
That came from deep within;
It wasn't hard to realize,
That the Lord was her dearest friend.

She now abides with God above,
On Heaven's wondrous shore;
Where not a hurt or heartache find,
Nor sadness anymore.

So, when we think of this dear one,
Who made our life so grand;
Remember that the day will come,
When we'll meet in glory land.

There'll be no time of parting,
No time of death and fears;
We'll live forever with Jesus,
In that land without tears.

07/25/2005 Nancy Horton-Liberty Baptist Church, Pueblo, CO

~ Steven R. Thacker ~

I'M HOME AT LAST

I look to the mount where God abides,
He cares for my pain and never leaves my side.

He watches over my bed of grief,
And holds my head while I sleep.

Though days turn into weeks and weeks to years,
His love is constant and He calms my fears.

The day will come when my life will pass,
And I'll have no more pain in this bed at last.

I'll leave this world and my loved ones dear,
To enter a land where there will be no more tears.

So, weep if you must, but your grief will pass,
Just think of me, "I'm home at last."

07/19/1993 In Memory of Jim Tolbert. Blessed Hope Bapt. Church, Spgfld, OH

HOME

Those burdens I carried are all now past,
I praise the Lord, for I'm home at last.

11/27/11

~ Steven R. Thacker ~

IN HIS CARE

She walked in gentle grace,
Along her earthly trail;
And trusted in her Savior's love,
For she knew He would never fail.

Her road was long and useful,
She cared for others so;
And knew that soon she'd be with God,
Though she hated to let you go.

And now she's gone above,
His joy forever share;
No longer will she suffer here,
For now she's in His care.

And now from Heaven's grandeur,
She sees you here below;
And hopes that you will trust in God,
As she did years ago.

07/24/2004 In Memory of Dora Baker Liberty Baptist Church, Pueblo, CO

GOD'S KEEPING

God keeps when the sky is cloudy,
And He keeps when the day is clear;
He keeps when I am cheerful,
And when my heart is full of fear.

11/31/11

~ Steven R. Thacker ~

"NANNY"

She walked in grace and beauty,
With care in every part;
She was always there to lend a hand,
With a willing and loving heart.

She prayed for all her family,
That they might walk with God;
She wanted to know they'd join her,
On Heaven's golden sod.

Through sickness, hurt and even pain,
She always seemed to smile;
You would find it hard to know,
That she was in a trial.

Nanny gave us so much more,
Then she had taken in;
She was a sweet and precious soul,
A kind and loving friend.

Heaven will be much sweeter,
When she arrives on shore;
But we will find a painful loss,
Of that one we so adored.

Though she has gone to glory,
And we find an empty chair;
We know that when this life is gone,
We'll meet her over there.

2006 To Nanny (Virginia) Garvin, Blessed Hope Baptist, Springfield, OH

~ Steven R. Thacker ~

OUR FRIEND

His laughter filled the room,
His kindness cradled all;
He had a way to make you feel,
Like you were ten feet tall.

He liked to speak of automobiles,
That he had traded through the years;
He liked to speak of his loving wife,
Through laughter, love and tears.

He always carried a smile,
Upon his rugged face;
He wouldn't show the pain he felt,
Instead he showed God's grace.

Jim loved and cared for family true,
His heart would overflow;
As often he would speak of them,
Though his feelings were hard to show.

2004 In memory of Jim Shubert—Liberty Baptist Church Pueblo, CO.

FRIENDSHIP

Friendships should not be misused,
They are precious from the start;
They are precious like a gentle breeze from God,
And should be guarded with the heart.

11/31/11

~ Steven R. Thacker ~

QUESTIONS

Why do the questions alarm my soul,
Err since I gave to You control?

I trust in You and have no doubt,
That whatever the conflict You'll bring me out.

I want to learn so much from You,
But my patience runs quite short, tis true.

I lay myself upon my bed,
With all these scriptures in my head.

And questions pour from my soul,
Like rushing streams and waters flow.

I take the time of loving friends,
And pour out questions again and again.

Now my head is true at rest,
And all those questions You have blest.

For in Your arms I now am fine,
With no more questions to clutter my mind.

6/10/1994 In memory of Joe Rouse, Blessed Hope Baptist Church, Spgfld, OH.

I WONDER

I wonder why we worry, and fret throughout the day;
For one day soon our Lord will come, to take us all away.

11/27/11

~ Steven R. Thacker ~

REMEMBER, I'LL MEET YOU IN THE SKY

I cross through darkness from this life,
To a land of great release;
My mortal frame removed from fears,
In this land of perfect peace.

I leave behind loved ones dear,
Who shared with me my load;
Though they with sadness on their face,
I share in Christ's abode.

If I could send but one regret,
To you I love so dear;
I think that it would be the hurt,
Of all your fallen tears.

Weep not because of the joys we've had,
And the friendships we have known;
For all these things will be enhanced,
Around our Father's throne.

And remember that our parting,
Is only for a time;
For our hearts and lives will meet again,
When the cords of heaven chime.

So, keep in mind, dear friends so true,
When your hearts give out a sigh;
That when the trumpet sounds above,
I'll meet you in the sky.

7/10/1994 In Memory of Paul Kreider, Blessed Hope Baptist, Spgfld, OH

~ Steven R. Thacker ~

SHE WALKED IN PEACE

She walked in peace,
With gentle grace;
With joy in her heart,
And a smile upon her face.

She had a drive,
And a zest for life;
She was a wonderful mother,
And a loving wife.

She enjoyed her family,
They made her life so sweet;
She had no regrets,
Because her life was complete.

And though she has gone,
And taken her flight;
We will miss her sweet smile,
And her guiding light.

But soon one day,
On Heaven's bright shore;
We'll meet her again,
And part no more.

12/16/2004 to Ray Baker Liberty Baptist Church, Pueblo, CO

WALKING WITH JESUS

When walking with Jesus, the way is clear;
He removes all doubt, and calms the fears.

11/27/11

~ Steven R. Thacker ~

SHE WAS A SOLDIER

Alma was a soldier,
Who held to God's own hand;
She trusted in her loving Lord,
Through smooth or sinking sand.

She lived a life of trusting,
And knowing God was right;
There never seemed to be a doubt,
Though rough may be her flight.

She suffered much with sickness,
Though few would ever know;
She wasn't one to speak of pain,
She wanted Christ to show.

She served the Lord with gladness,
As a pastor's loving wife;
Her service was to young and old,
As she touched them with her life.

God gave to us a blessing,
In this dear saint of love;
But now she's in her Savior's home,
In Heaven up above.

6/20/1995 Alma Yonker, Blessed Hope Baptist Church, Spgfld, OH

THE ONE WHO LOVES US

The One who loves us through every day,
Will one day take us home to stay.
11/28/11

~ Steven R. Thacker ~

SHE WAS SPECIAL

Nina gave to each of us,
A special kind of joy;
The memory of this precious soul,
Cannot in time destroy.

I loved her clever ways,
As she lighted up a room;
She always made a smile appear,
When ones heart was filled with gloom.

She often spoke of Jim,
And how she missed him so;
She knew the day was coming soon,
When to his side she'd go.

Nina leaves a group of friends,
And loved ones here below;
But on the other side with God,
There is much more you know.

Although we'd like to keep her here,
And never say farewell;
We know she's in a better place,
With God in Heaven to dwell.

So, say goodbye and spend your grief,
And let dear Nina be;
For soon one day—if we've trusted God,
Her face again we'll see.

1993 In Memory of Nina Tolbert, Blessed Hope Baptist Church, Spgfld, OH

~ Steven R. Thacker ~

SWEET PEACE FOR THEE

Tears will pass away,
On that lovely golden shore;
And all the pain that life had brought,
Will trouble us no more.

Our lives will then be all complete,
When loved ones we shall see;
No more will tears fall from our eyes,
Just sweet peace for thee.

The Savior waits to walk with me,
With those nail-prints in His hands;
His face is the one I long to see,
In that wondrous distant land.

But while I finish up my course,
And I travel here below;
My loved ones who have died in Christ,
I'll see again I know.

4/1/1997 To my friend Bill Haney, Blessed Hope Baptist Church, Spgfld, OH

PEACE

Peace is often hoped for,
And we long to see it shown;
But only in the arms of God,
Can peace be truly known.

11/31/11

~ Steven R. Thacker ~

THE REASON WHY

We miss their talk of kindness,
The smile upon their face;
We miss their gentle words of love,
And that loving warm embrace.

Though that loved one is no longer here,
It will cause us grief and pain;
And though we cry and plead with God,
They can't come back again.

But we can find the peace we need,
Within the Savior's care;
And know that when our time has come,
We'll find them waiting there.

And though we question the reason why,
That they were taken from this life;
We must find sweet comfort in God's embrace,
That He knows what's truly right.

03/10/06 Liberty Baptist Church, Pueblo, Colorado

WHY WORRY?

Why should we worry,
When God is in our heart?
We only need to trust Him,
And to simply do our part.

11/30/11

~ Steven R. Thacker ~

THE TIME SHE SPENT WITH ME

Carrie was one who had a special gift,
That others may not see;
I would come to visit and to encourage her,
But it was she who would encourage me.

I loved to sit and talk with her,
She spoke with purpose and truth;
And she knew though her life may be trying,
She has a Savior to lead her through.

She had no doubts about her life with God,
And of her family that she loved so dear;
She knew that her Master had a plan,
And she sought it so strong and clear.

This dear lady that I loved so true,
Has left her mark you see;
For I've been blessed more than you can know,
Through those times she spent with me.
1/5/2003 Carrie Harvel Victory Baptist Church, Jamestown, OH

LOVING HANDS

God wants us to be at hand,
When others need some cheer;
It helps them face the hurts in life,
When they know that someone's near.
11/4/2011

~ Steven R. Thacker ~

UNTIL WE MEET AGAIN

She traveled through this life of ours,
Not very long it seems;
She walked in loving kindness here,
And shared with us her dreams.

It's hard to fathom life at all,
Without her presence here;
Though life goes on with family close,
There's still that empty chair.

We find our minds in recent past,
And all we've said and done;
We fret about the wasted time,
That never again will come.

But I believe that she would say,
"Don't worry your life away;
Just trust in God's only Son,
That you might come my way."

For in His hands she gave her life,
So many years ago;
That she might have a home above,
In the peace of Heaven's glow.

May God give us discernment,
Until we meet above;
And walk in realms of glory,
In that land of purest love.

11/17/2006 In Memory of Teresa Stokely, Liberty Baptist Church, Pueblo, CO

~ Steven R. Thacker ~

SHE WAS A WONDER

Betty was a wonder,
And a joy for all to see;
For hers was one of warmth and grace,
And her heart was kind and free.

As I would wonder back in time,
And her precious face I'd see;
I recall her loving smile,
Whenever she greeted me.

She loved her husband greatly,
And her children strong and true;
But most of all she loved her Lord,
And she knew He loved her too.

For one sweet day she gave to Him,
And entrance in her heart;
And from that day she stayed on course,
Never to depart.

So, while we grieve the absence,
Of her presence and her love;
We can rest assured that she's at rest,
With her Savior up above.

02/10/2011 In memory of his loving Betty Burns

WHEN DEATH IS MINE

When death is mine and life is past,
I'll praise the Lord for I'll be home at last.

11/28/11

~ Steven R. Thacker ~

A GENTLE MAN

Jim was one of greatness,
In the army of his Lord;
He walked in peace with all he met,
With a gentle sweet accord.

When first I met this precious man,
In the church where God had shown;
He met me with a loving smile,
And the assurance that I was not alone.

My family felt more at ease,
Because of his friendship true;
He always was there to lend a hand,
In the work we had to do.

Jim was always busy,
In that church he loved so well;
In the church I would hear him working,
More oft then I could tell.

I'll never forget this gentle man,
With his loving and tender ways;
'Til one day soon we'll meet again,
In that land of endless days.

08/3/2009 In Memory of Jim Walters, Liberty Baptist Church, Pueblo, CO

~ Steven R. Thacker ~

GOD'S SERVANT

Clarence was a servant,
Strong and true;
He trusted his Lord,
His whole life through.

He served as a pastor,
Most of his life;
And God had blessed him,
With a loving wife.

They served together,
Through good times and bad;
But never a whisper,
Of those troubles they had.

The message of salvation,
And the forgiveness of sin;
He would preach with power,
Again and again.

Though he now is gone,
To Heaven above;
We shall never forget,
This servant of love.

His message was clear,
And now his mission complete;
As he sits in peace,
At his Savior's dear feet.

09/15/2009 In Memory of Rev. Clarence Yonker Blessed Hope Bapt., Spgfld, OH

~ Steven R. Thacker ~

HIS SMILE

He stands at the door,
And opens with such care;
It's always good to see,
That Dick is always there.

His sweet and gentle spirit,
Would always be displayed;
As he shook a hand or gave a smile,
In his kind and loving way.

He loved his family true,
And walked with God above;
His life was an open sign,
Of a man in a journey of love.

It's hard now to see,
That vacant place;
Where he served for years,
With that smiling face.

So, we must say goodbye,
To this brother we love;
Until that sweet day,
When we meet above.

In that great day,
In that distant land;
We'll see his smile,
And we'll shake his hand.

12/10/2009 In Memory of Richard Hayes, Blessed Hope Baptist, Spgfld, OH

~ Steven R. Thacker ~

HER SMILE

She walked in sweet reflection,
Of a Savior strong and true;
Though her health had been a burden,
Her Lord would bring her through.

But the smile she always carried,
And the joy she did embrace;
Should give us all the courage,
To seek our Savior's face.

She loved her husband greatly,
And all her family too;
But she trusted most in Jesus,
With a heart that's strong and true.

Now when we think of Sue,
And that smile upon her face;
We think of her in loving arms,
In that land of amazing grace.

2/9/10 In Memory of Sue Penix, Freedom Baptist Temple, Xenia OH

A PLEASANT SMILE

A smile costs us nothing,
And can often change a life;
As it lifts the veil of sadness,
From that one who is filled with strife.

05/22/2011

~ Steven R. Thacker ~

I REACH BEYOND THIS DAY

I reach beyond this day,
To move beyond the tears;
Of the joy that was my yesterday,
And the wonder of those years.

I find myself awaking,
In the silence of my night;
I feel the pillow beside my head,
And recall her heavenly flight.

I whisper to my Savior,
For that strength I need again;
"Please help me in my sorrow,
For on You I must depend."

And with the gentle breath of God,
Like the brush of Angel's wings;
He gently takes my trembling hand,
And helps my heart to sing.

"The sorrow felt today," He says,
"Is only for a while;
For one day soon, my child,
You once again will smile."

"For your love is yonder waiting,
With her hand outstretched to you;
As she waits to guide you on to God,
In that land beyond the blue.

So, rest my child and trust Me,
And cherish every day;
For those nights will not be so threatening,
When you turn your eyes My way."

For real joy is not in yesterday,
And the years that are your past;
They're in that future Home above,
Where sweet joy will forever last.

2010 To my friend, Dan Penix, Freedom Baptist Temple, Xenia, OH
~ Steven R. Thacker ~

IN GOD'S HEAVEN

We gather in this quiet place,
With memories so very clear;
We think of Rose who has gone above,
This one we loved so dear.

She's taken loves sweet journey,
To that land beyond the blue;
And now awaits with loved ones dear,
For the arrival of me and you.

There was a time in years gone by,
That she prepared for this fateful day;
As she trusted in a Savior's love,
To take her sins away.

She now enjoys a freedom,
With a life of joy and peace;
As she leaves the bounds of this earth,
And finds God's sweet release.

Though our hearts will feel the burden,
Of the absence of her embrace;
We know the day is coming soon,
When again we'll see her face.

When the bounds of earth release us,
And we make our journey too;
To that land where Rose awaits us,
In God's Heaven beyond the blue.

02/2/2010 In Memory of Rose Cayton, Grace Baptist Church, Newark OH

~ Steven R. Thacker ~

HE LOVED

He loved his Ginny and all could see,
As he had back at the start;
That from the time she walked the aisle,
He held her in his heart.

Don also loved to fish,
And he loved his Ginny's pies;
And he always had a story to tell,
With that twinkle in his eyes.

He cherished his Jesus,
And he loved his family true;
And now in Heaven's endless days,
He'll wait for me and you.

So, now as he is absent,
And his spirit has gone above;
We'll cherish all the memories,
And we'll remember how he loved.

Soon the days of waiting,
Will swiftly pass us by;
And we'll see our precious friend again,
In that land beyond the sky.

03/27/2009 Memory of Don White past member Victory Bapt. Jamestown, OH

~ Steven R. Thacker ~

HE WALKED IN SADNESS

He walked the path of sadness,
Where tears would often flow;
He hid the hurt within his heart,
For peace he could not know.

But then one day he turned to God,
So He would free from sin;
He gave to God his broken life,
For he longed for peace within.

And then the Lord brought victory,
Where once defeat had been;
He now would love and serve the Lord,
For He's now his dearest friend.

And though his voice was raspy,
And his tone was often firm;
Deep within this precious man,
Beat a heart that God had turned.

For once his life was hindered,
And burdened down with strife;
The Lord abides now within,
As He gave this man new life.

One great thing about this man,
And this we all did know;
If you ever wondered what he thought,
He sure would tell you so.

This man was such a joy to me,
A friend that stood so dear;
He found it hard to share his heart,
And hated to show a tear.

~ Steven R. Thacker ~

He told me often about his love,
For his family around him here;
And all the joy they brought to him,
On those days of want and fear.

He needed to be with Nancy,
In that land beyond compare;
And though he loved his family so,
He longed to meet her there.

And so today we say goodbye,
To this brother strong and true;
We know the day is coming soon,
When we'll meet beyond the blue.

02/21/2006 In Memory of Billie Bob Horton Liberty Bapt. Church, Pueblo, CO

~ Steven R. Thacker ~

A SERVANT STRONG AND TRUE

He chose a course of faith and love,
A servant strong and true;
He adored his wife of many years,
And he cherished his children too.

Bill loved the church with all his heart,
And would always be in place;
To greet the folks as they came in,
With a warm welcome and a smiling face.

Now with the boiler at the church,
That would see Bill's special care;
It seemed that he was the only one,
To coax it to put out warm air.

We find it hard to think of life,
Without this man so dear;
We will miss his words of comfort,
And his way of giving cheer.

But one day soon in realms above,
We'll take him by the hand;
And know the joy of fellowship sweet,
As we unite in that distant land.

Where Bill will be enjoying,
A place of God's perfect care;
For there will never be a need,
Of a boiler over there.

05/7/2011 In Memory of Wilburn (Bill) Garvin Blessed Hope Baptist, Spfld, OH.

~ Steven R. Thacker ~

HE WALKS THROUGH LIFE

He walks through life,
This gentle man;
Holding tight,
To the Savior's hand.

His kindness too,
Was always shone;
And no better friend,
Could there be known.

I guess he learned,
To be that way;
By following his Lord,
Each and every day.

And when his journey,
On earth is complete;
He will find himself,
At his Savior's feet.

For he walks through life,
This gentle man;
Holding tight,
To his Savior's hand.

3/16/2007 To my friend, Cecil Mundy, Blessed Hope Bapt Church, Spgfld, OH

~ Steven R. Thacker ~

A KIND AND LOVING MAN

His life was one of kindness,
A sweet and loving man;
He loved to sing and praise the Lord,
And to lend a helping hand.

He loved his wife and children,
And his grandchildren with all his heart;
He loved the church he served,
Where he would always do his part.

Bruce was one of laughter,
And jokes he loved to share;
It was clear for all to see,
He was one who truly cared.

But the body he was housed in,
Had imprisoned his very life;
Each day for him was a struggle,
With its pain and constant strife.

But one day came a summons,
That was sent from God above;
He opened up those prison bars,
And embraced him in His love.

Bruce is now in Glory,
With loved ones who've gone before;
And the pain and hurt that he had known,
Will trouble him no more.

So, now this kind and loving man,
Is in the arms of God above;
Surrounded by God's presence,
And at peace within His love.

2/12 In memory of Bruce Spencer, Bible Bapt. Church, Xenia, Oh.

~ Steven R. Thacker ~

SECTION 4

Poems dedicated to my loving wife, and others.

STANDING GUARD

Though Satan try to besiege this home,
To hinder all within;
I want to do my best for God,
To keep my home from sin.

Though fierce may be the conflict,
And long may be the strife;
I'll stand on guard of my home,
And protect it with my life.

For my children are an inheritance,
Sent down from God above;
They show me in so many ways,
Their sweet and constant love.

And God has sent into my life,
A wife so sweet and dear;
A mate that always walks with me,
Through all these many years.

So, I must stand on guard you see,
With commitment from the start;
And keep the Devil outside these walls,
Of this home close to my heart.

1993

~ Steven R. Thacker ~

A LOCKET OF LOVE

This locket of love,
That is now in your care;
Is a treasure that we trust,
We will both always share.

For within this heart of gold,
That was chosen with such care;
You will find two special guys,
Whose life you now share.

It's our hope that in those times,
When you show it to your friends;
You can tell them of a special love,
That we know will never end.

So, may each time that you wear,
This locket and its chain;
You'll be reminded of our love,
And that feeling will always remain.

2005 Christmas To my Debby Jo with love from your two guys, Steve and Cody

TO MY LOVE

As the rain flows down from heaven,
And the morning brings its dew;
There'll never be a time on earth,
When I will not love you.

1998 To my Debby Jo

~ Steven R. Thacker ~

OUR CODY

Cody came into our home,
From a place of deep despair;
His life was one of sad neglect,
One absent of loving care.

So, God with His loving grace,
Did search for a proper home;
Where Cody would be cared for,
In a place he could call his own.

God opened up a heart so true,
And placed this baby there;
So Debby couldn't help but love,
This child who had no care.

My heart is often saddened,
For those who gave up in the midst of strife;
For they will never understand,
What they've missed in Cody's life.

For Cody is a wondrous child,
Who brings joy to every day;
He gives so much to enrich our life,
In so many countless ways.

So, we need to thank our Savior,
For this gift we love so dear;
For Cody is a wondrous joy,
He blesses throughout the year.

May God give us the courage,
To raise him with loving care;
And give him the security,
Of parents that will always be there.

11/21/2002

~ Steven R. Thacker ~

THE WONDER OF CHILDREN

The wonder of children,
As they run and sing;
The wonder of children,
And the joy they bring.

The wonder of children,
How fast they grow;
The wonder of children,
And all the love they show.

So, cherish those years,
For they will not last;
And the wonder of children,
Will then be past.

2009

~ Steven R. Thacker ~

TO MY PRINCESS

I love you more today,
Then I ever have before;
And it's a sure and certain bet,
That tomorrow I'll love you more.
1995 To my loving wife, Debby Jo

~ Steven R. Thacker ~

MEMORIES

Lois is a mother and a grandmother,
With a love so strong and true;
She embraces all the memories,
And the years they brought her through.

She has seen the face of sadness,
In the loss of those who've died;
And also in the gladness,
Of her family by her side.

She now awaits the visits,
Of her children now and then;
And will cherish each phone call,
With a loving and gentle grin.

But the one thing that brings comfort,
And the thought that is so grand;
Is the knowledge of her trust in God,
And she is safe in her Master's hand.

For her Daddy was a preacher,
He taught of Jesus' love;
She learned to place her trust in Christ,
And gain Heaven up above.

08/26/2011 To my mother-in-law, Lois Summers Steiner

~ Steven R. Thacker ~

DEBBY'S HAND

I wasn't the first one to want her,
I fought both long and hard;
For Debby was a beautiful girl,
And it kept me on my guard.

There were suitors who would taunt her,
With their words that seemed so grand;
But I was the lucky boy,
Who ended up with Debby's hand.

I still recall that wondrous day,
Though so many years have gone;
That wondrous day in God's sweet plan,
When we each became just one.

Our family and friends were gathered near,
In that church that stood so grand;
When, John, (her Grandpa) walked with her,
And gave me Debby's hand.

That hand has seen us through much strife,
In those early years gone past;
For it was only with her hand in mine,
That I knew our love would last.

~ Steven R. Thacker ~

Her hands were strong when children came,
As she wiped their tears away;
They still were strong in corrections need,
When they would try to stray.

Her hand was strong when tragedy came,
And God took our eldest son;
Though she spoke to God in words of love,
That this should not be done.

I praise the Lord for Debby's hand,
When times like these we'd know;
For she would be the strength I'd need,
As we still must onward go.

I know not what life has in store,
As we journey through this land;
But I know that I can face each one,
With the help of Debby's hand.

08/21/2005 To my loving wife, Debby Jo

~ Steven R. Thacker ~

MY DEBBY JO

The dream of my life,
Was granted long ago;
When God through his wondrous grace,
Gave to me my Debby Jo.

No man could ever hope to find,
A treasure such as she;
She shows her love in all she does,
She's such a blessing to me.

I can't begin to thank You, Lord,
If I had a thousand years;
She brings me love, peace and joy,
And calms my every fear.

I pray that God will grant to me,
The health and time to show;
How much I truly love my wife,
My precious Debby Jo.

2002 To my loving wife (just because)

~ Steven R. Thacker ~

THIS SPECIAL DAY

This special day,
Was set aside;
So busy men,
Might remember their bride.

So ladies of leisure,
Or work or play;
Might recall that lad,
Who stole their heart away.

And through my thoughts,
Of youth and cheer;
Might recall that day,
That we met, my dear.

My thoughts of you,
Is on every day;
I need no special reminder, Love,
Of how you stole my heart away.

I love you more,
Than from the start;
And I'll love you always,
With all my heart.

But so that I might,
More thoughtful be;
Here's a valentine,
To you from me.

2004 Valentine's Day from your loving husband, Steve

~ Steven R. Thacker ~

WITH DEBBY AT MY SIDE

The loving kiss of God's sweet grace,
Has blessed me through the years;
In the mate that He has given me,
Through heartache and often tears.

She never speaks of troubles sore,
Nor discomfort of the day;
But always near with helping hand,
To support me on my way.

In the work where God has led,
The road would often go;
To places far from home,
To folks we would not know.

Yet she would carry within her heart,
A joy that was so true;
That God could use those hands of clay,
To help and guide folks through.

What a wondrous joy to work for God,
In this place we now abide;
For peace is mine as on we go,
With Debby at my side.

6/27/2004 Happy 34th Anniversary from your loving husband, Steve

~ Steven R. Thacker ~

LOVE CAN NOT BE MEASURED

Love cannot be measured,
Not with a poet's pen;
And dreams cannot be understood,
Though tried by countless men.

True love is like a fountain,
That never shall run dry;
It fills the life with purpose,
And causes hearts to fly.

They fly above the burdens,
And soar above the strife;
For nothing brings such joy and peace,
As love within one's life.

01/25/2007

~ Steven R. Thacker ~

I LOVE YOU

I love you, Honey, with all my heart,
On this you can depend;
Though much of life with us may change,
My love will never end.

I often think of what your love,
Has meant to me through time;
And how I could place this truth,
Upon the written line.

So that all may see and know my heart,
And see God's grace so true;
Who gave to me a gift so great,
That precious gift of you.

To speak of all your wonders,
Your gentle sharing ways;
Would be too numerous for me to mention,
As the suns sweet golden rays.

When often I am troubled,
Or my illness has shown its dread;
I know that you are ever near,
To the place I lay my head.

I need not fear the darkness,
Nor a daytime filled with gloom;
For when my eyes regain their light,
You'll be there in my room.

You remind me of that constant love,
That God has given to man;
Throughout the ages ever strong,
As it flows from God's sweet hand.

~ Steven R. Thacker ~

My love for you is ever true,
As a rose upon its stem;
It offers up its life to you,
And draws its strength from Him.

As the rose will give its life,
To bring to you such peace;
I too would gladly give my life,
That your life might more increase.

The rose's peddles will one day fall,
From off its stem so high;
Be sure my love will constant be,
For my love will never die.

For you see our love is not the type,
That comes from life's demands;
It's from the portals up above,
A gift from God's own hands.

So, in this world of troubles, Dear,
And though this earth may slide;
I know that ours is such a love,
That will ever more abide.

So, take this note from my heart,
And hold it near your breast;
And keep in mind that no matter what,
That I've given to you my best.

Our bodies are but mortal clay,
And time will prove this true;
I thank my God for giving me,
The precious gift of you.

Yours forever, Steve

~ Steven R. Thacker ~

THIS FAMILY

Our children gave us joy,
All those years gone by;
Their wondrous glow in winter's snow,
And that twinkle in their eye.

And now the grandchildren,
With love so free;
They come right in,
And climb upon the knee.

I wonder back,
Across the years;
As we saw such joy,
And sometimes tears.

But I wouldn't trade,
This life of mine;
For any of the riches,
That man could find.

No, my wife and I,
Would never trade;
This family that we have,
And the memories that they've made.

So, I praise the Lord,
For this family of love;
He has given a gift,
That's from Heaven above.

02/16/2007

~ Steven R. Thacker ~

GOD HAS BLESSED

God has blessed this boy 'tis true;
With such a loving wife as you.

You're all of life and love to me;
And it's at your side I long to be.

Though sometimes miles would keep us apart;
You're always near within my heart.

So, when you find yourself alone;
And you question what is true.

Just remember, Debby, with all my heart;
I'll always be in love with you.
2007

THERE IS A LINE

There is a line,
That I speak that's true;
It's when I say,
That I love you.

I thank the Lord,
Each day I live;
For the wonder of you,
And the love you give.
2005

~ Steven R. Thacker ~

DAD

A rare and precious gift today,
Is in the Christian Dad;
Who fears not where the crowd may lead,
But remains in God's sweet hand.

He watches o'er his loving home,
That God has given him;
And strives to keep them safe from sin,
For Satan may buffet them.

He takes his roll with sacred trust,
And prays both night and day;
That God would keep them safe from harm,
And that his children would not stray.

So, if you have within your home,
A father strong and true;
Be sure to say, "I love you, Dad,
For all the things you do."

Date unknown

~ Steven R. Thacker ~

THAT NURSERY SONG

The years of children,
How fast they're gone;
Those teetering years,
And that nursery song.

They move from blocks,
On their bedroom floor;
To riding a bike,
And so much more.

They learn to read,
And add and write;
And some fear that monster,
When they say goodnight.

They want to be big,
When they're still very small;
And they call out your name,
When they slip and fall.

Too soon the years,
Of cradle and play pen;
Give way to those ballgames,
And that "special" friend.

Too soon those questions,
Of yesteryear;
Give way to the quandaries,
That we don't wish to hear.

Yes, one day those babies,
Will be grown and gone;
And it's to their children you sing,
That nursery song.

09/18/2009

~ Steven R. Thacker ~

REDEEM THE TIME

Those about us,
We seldom see;
Though they bless our lives,
Time will too often flee.

Too soon time will pass,
And the years will go by;
And it's then we look back,
And grieve with a sigh.

For those we love,
Will one day die;
And we look back and see,
That the years had sped by.

We cannot go back,
To regain those lost years;
No matter the heartache,
And no matter the tears.

So, now is the time,
To love and show care;
For one day we'll see,
That they will not be there.

Hold to their hand,
And bring them in tight;
And when they are gone,
Everything will be alright.

09/21/2009

~ Steven R. Thacker ~

I PRAISE YOU LORD

O, breath of God,
O, Lord Divine;
I praise You for,
This love of mine.

It seems that though,
The years pass by;
It only grows,
With each passing sigh.

I see around me,
Most every day;
Sad cold looks,
And hearts so gray.

For they have lost,
Their mate so true;
And now each day,
Just leaves them blue.

So, thank you, Lord,
And I praise you so;
For this love so true,
For my sweet Debby Jo.

O, breath of God,
O, Lord Divine;
I praise You for,
This love of mine.
03/24/1999

~ Steven R. Thacker ~

A TREASURE

She walks in grace and beauty,
All can clearly see;
That she's trusted God for salvation,
For all eternity.

She has a zest for living,
And a warm and gentle smile;
I could spend the whole day long,
Reminiscing all the while.

She has a love for her grandchildren,
And her family young and old;
There are her memories of her siblings,
Oh the stories she has told.

She speaks of her dear husband,
And her loving Mom and Dad;
The years back on the homestead,
And the times both good and bad.

But the thing I treasure most,
As I see her now and again;
Is that we are more than relatives,
We're close and loving friends.

I know the time is coming,
When she'll leave her house of clay;
And go where God and loved ones abide,
In that land of the endless day.

09/23/2011 To my Precious Aunt, Ruth Messer

~ Steven R. Thacker ~

GRIP HIS HAND

When walking in the darkness,
And fear obscures the trail;
Just trust in Him, dear child of God,
The One who never fails.

He walked with Paul and Silas,
And Daniel in the den;
Just rest in Him, dear child of God,
For you can always trust in Him.

So, when the way is uncertain,
And you wonder in the night;
Just trust in Him, dear child of God,
And grip His hand real tight.

October 18, 2011

~ Steven R. Thacker ~

LIFE FOR ALL

God has granted life for all,
Who will respond to the Savior's call?
11/27/11

HEAVEN SENT

God gave to me a friend,
Who is thoughtful, kind and true;
He seeks the Lord to guide him,
In the work He'd have him do.

Whenever the need arises,
And one needs a helping hand;
You'll always find he's first in line,
With a heart that's oh so grand.

God has bless him with a gift,
To those who cannot pay;
He wants the Lord to use him,
In so many different ways.

Yes, Roger is a blessing,
And has been for many years;
We have shared in times of laughter,
And sometimes in shedding tears.

But if I could speak a simple phrase,
To tell what he has meant;
I guess I'd have to say to you,
That he is 'Heaven Sent'.

10/19/11 To my friend, Roger Davis, Springfield, OH

~ Steven R. Thacker ~

HEAVEN COMPLETE

One night I heard a whisper,
From Heaven's distant shore;
He said my time had ended,
And my struggles would be no more.

I closed my eyes and wondered,
What would my future be?
As I rest within my Savior's care,
For His face I long to see.

I awakened in such splendor,
With glory all around;
The streets of gold that glittered,
Oh, such sights that I have found.

My Grandma came to greet me,
With a smile so strong and true;
Mom and Dad was also there,
And Aunt Bea was nearby too.

I also saw my cousin Rod,
Who I thought was lost in sin;
He must have trusted in God's grace,
And turned his face toward Him.

Grandpa and Grandma Steiner came,
And how I loved to hear them speak;
Then Corey came and hugged his daddy's neck,
And kissed me on the cheek.

~ Steven R. Thacker ~

With all the glories about me,
And my Savior standing near;
I had a longing deep within,
For I missed your presence, Dear.

We've spent so many years, my love,
Upon this earth below;
With children, home, and family,
And all those joys we've known.

So, even though in Heaven,
In the midst of God's sweet grace;
I'll still possess a longing, Dear,
To see your loving face.

So, I'll wait for you in Heaven,
Across that golden strand;
Then you and I can take a walk,
And journey hand in hand.

For Heaven would not be Heaven,
Until you're there with me;
So, I'll hang around that golden gate,
Until your face I see.

10/19/2011 To my precious Debby Jo

~ Steven R. Thacker ~

CHOICES

We all have choices in life,
To live or to die;
To give or to take,
To quit or to try.

We all have needs in life,
We need love and loyalty;
We need joy and peace,
We need God's love to set us free.

But whether choices or needs,
Or whether peace or love;
There's only one place they both are found,
With our Father up above.
11/5/2011

DREAMS

Dreams in the night may be fearful,
And our clouds may turn to gray;
But when life is in our Savior's hand,
He'll move those clouds away.
11/5/2011

~ Steven R. Thacker ~

CALMNESS OF SPIRIT

Calmness of spirit is a gift from God,
It holds our vessel true;
With our lives in God's sweet care,
He'll see us safely through.

Through the hurts and the heartaches,
And through our painful past;
He'll give a life of lasting joy,
And a calmness that will last.

11/5/2011

HE HOLDS

He holds me close, He holds me right;
He's present in the day, and also in the night.

11/5/2011

~ Steven R. Thacker ~